Scarlet Ibis

Also by Gill Lewis:

Sky Hawk
White Dolphin
Moon Bear

Scarlet Ibis

Gill Lewis

OXFORD
UNIVERSITY PRESS

OXFORD
UNIVERSITY PRESS

Great Clarendon Street, Oxford OX2 6DP

Oxford University Press is a department of the University of Oxford.
It furthers the University's objective of excellence in research, scholarship,
and education by publishing worldwide. Oxford is a registered trade mark of
Oxford University Press in the UK and in certain other countries

Database right Oxford University Press (maker)

First published 2014

British Library Cataloguing in Publication Data

Data available

ISBN: 978-0-19-279355-3

1 3 5 7 9 10 8 6 4 2

Printed in Great Britain

Paper used in the production of this book is a natural,
recyclable product made from wood grown in sustainable forests.
The manufacturing process conforms to the environmental
regulations of the country of origin.

For Big Nose,
who found it and brought it home.

CHAPTER 1

'Be careful, Red,' I say.

He looks at me, his eyes wide, his red hair lit up by the setting sun.

I stare at the space between us. 'I can see crocodiles.'

'Caimans,' he says. 'We're not in Africa.'

'OK, caimans,' I say.

Red watches them. He sees them moving beneath the water, their bodies leaving ripples and trails of bubbles on the surface.

'Come on,' I say. 'There'll be no time for a story.'

Red's hands clench and unclench in small fists.

He's working it out, planning every move in his mind. He has to take five steps across the lagoon of green carpet, only letting the soles of his feet touch the brown threadbare patches before he reaches safety. I keep my fingers crossed he gets it right first time. If he gets it wrong he'll make himself start all the way back in the bathroom with brushing his teeth again. Last night we had to go through it all three times. I sit on the beanbag next to his bed and pull the covers back. His fleece blanket is patterned with peacock feathers. Red takes five steps and leaps into bed. He turns to his left and then his right and presses his hands together beneath his cheek. I pull his blanket up around him so all I can see is his hair on the pillow and his eyes peeping out.

'So which story is it tonight?' I say.

'Caroni Swamp,' he says.

I smile because there is only ever one story. I dim his side-lamp and begin. 'Some day,' I say, 'we'll find ourselves an aeroplane and fly up into the big blue sky. We'll be like birds. We'll fly above the roads and houses, above Big Ben, The Eye and London Zoo. We'll fly across the whole Atlantic Ocean, all the way to Trinidad.'

'What then?' says Red.

'We'll take a little boat out on the Caroni Swamp,' I say.

'Just you and me?' says Red.

'Just you and me,' I say.

The corners of Red's eyes crinkle as he smiles. He's seeing the deep green waters, and tangle of the mangrove trees.

Scarlet Ibis

'And we'll wait,' I say. 'We'll wait for the sun to sink, turning the mountains of the Northern Range deep blue.'

'Just you and me?' says Red.

'Just you and me,' I say. 'And as the light is leaving the sky, we'll watch them coming in their hundreds and thousands. We'll watch them settle in the trees like bright red lanterns as darkness falls.'

Red pulls his blanket tighter around him. 'And we'll always be together?'

'Always,' I say. 'Just you and me in that little boat, as evening falls, watching the scarlet ibis flying back to the Caroni Swamp.'

'Night Red,' I whisper.

I stand up to pull his curtains closed. I pull them slowly. I don't want to scare the pigeon outside on the narrow window ledge. She's sitting on a nest of tangled sticks and plastic, her pale grey wings are folded, and her head is tucked close to her chest in sleep. Beneath her, hidden under her soft feathers, lies the small white egg that Red has been watching every day.

Red opens one eye and peeps at me. 'It still hasn't hatched.'

'It will,' I say.

'When?'

I lean in close to him. 'When it's ready,' I whisper. 'Now, shh! Go to sleep.'

I sit with Red while his eyes close and I watch him drift into sleep. His tight little frown relaxes and makes him look four years old again, even though he's nearly eight. I fold his school clothes on the chair, pile his Lego back in the box, and pack it away. I sit back on the beanbag and stroke his hair. I want to stay like this, with Red. I don't want anything to change. I don't even want to think of what tomorrow might bring.

'Scarlet!'

Mum's in the kitchen, calling me. She's banging cupboard doors and sliding drawers open and shut.

'Scarlet, where are you?'

I pull Red's door closed behind me and go and find Mum. She's in her dressing gown and slippers. A cup of tea sits on the table. Her long dark hair falls in knots and tangles on her shoulders.

'I didn't hear you get up,' I say. 'There's half a pie in the oven for you.'

Mum opens another drawer and rummages through the clutter of keys and rubber bands and the stuff we don't know where else to put. She scatters things on the work surface beside her.

'What are you looking for?' I say.

Mum pulls out the whole drawer and tips it on to the table. 'My tablets. Have you seen them?'

'I locked them in the bathroom cupboard.'

Mum glares at me. 'What d'you do that for?'

'We have to keep them somewhere Red can't reach them. Mrs Gideon will check up on that again. She's coming tomorrow. Don't you remember?'

'Oh!' says Mum. She frowns and pushes a strand of hair back from her face. 'You mean the Penguin?'

I see her mouth twitch in a smile and I smile too. Mrs Gideon is the social worker who comes to spy on us. Red calls them all penguins. I know what he means. They're like the penguins at the zoo, the way they strut about, yabbering and poking their beaks into everything.

Mrs Gideon always asks me to call her Jo. She wants to be on first name terms so we can 'build a relationship of mutual trust'. But I call her Mrs Gideon, because I don't want her thinking she's any friend of mine.

'She'll be here at two,' I say. I watch Mum closely. She's been in bed all day and I know she'll be awake all night, just like last night. She'll be pacing in her room or sitting at the window staring out across the city, listening to trains rattling through the station. She'll probably be back in bed tomorrow afternoon.

Mum nods. 'I'll make sure I'm in,' she says.

'Fine,' I say. But it's not fine really because it's not as if Mum will be out. She's only leaves the flat to get her tablets and her cigarettes. I just want her to be up and dressed when Mrs Gideon comes.

I turn the oven on and shake some frozen peas into a pan while Mum finds her tablets. At least she's taking them. It's a good sign. A very good sign. Maybe tomorrow will be OK.

Mum sits down, takes three tablets, and gulps them down with a swig of tea. 'You've done the washing!' she says.

I sit down next to her. 'I did the sheets, though they won't be dry by tomorrow. I've vacuumed too,' I say. 'You know how fussy penguins can be!'

Mum's leans across and puts her hand on mine. 'We'll be OK Scarlet, don't you worry.'

I smile and feel warm deep down inside. She's looking at me. I'm not invisible to her today. 'Red found another feather,' I say.

Mum takes another sip of tea. 'What sort?'

'Magpie tail feather,' I say. 'A really long one. It's jet

Scarlet Ibis

black but shines bright green in the sunlight. He found it in the playground. I could get him to show you if you like.'

Mum's smiling but she's not really listening. 'Why don't we do something tonight, just you and me? We could watch a DVD,' she says. 'Would you like that?'

I nod, but think of the homework I have to do by tomorrow. 'You set it up. I'll put the bins out first,' I say.

I pull the full bag from the bin and check the fridge for old food. I chuck away a lump of mouldy cheese that Mrs Gideon might use as evidence against us. Last time she came, she offered to fetch milk from the fridge for Mum's cup of tea. But I know she was just snooping. It's what she does. I see her eyes scanning our flat, trying to find something to put in her report. There's only a pint of milk and half a loaf of bread in the fridge now. Maybe she'll accuse Mum of starving us. It's hard to get it right.

'Won't be long,' I yell.

I lug the bin bag down the stairwell, my feet echoing in the empty space. The lift is broken again and I hate using it anyway. It always smells of beer and wee and you never know who's going to get in it with you. Still, I don't mind the stairs and I like living in the top flat. Eight floors up, we can see across the station and the trains and all the other houses. Red pretends we're birds and our flat is our nest.

It feels that way to me too.

We're safe up here.

Out of reach.

I jump down three steps at a time. The TV blares from the Kanwars' flat on floor six. I can hear Pat and Brian arguing from floor one. The ground floor flat is silent, boarded up and out of use. Outside, Chalkie and his gang are on their bikes doing turns and spins along the pavement. I keep in the shadows and walk around to the back of the flats and sling the bin-bag in the skip. Beyond the wall lie the trains and doughnut stalls in the station. The smell of diesel fumes and sugar mix together and fill the night air. The sun has set, and beyond the orange haze of streetlights I can just see the stars. It's another good sign. Another very good sign.

'*Titanic*,' says Mum.

'OK,' I say. It's her favourite film. I get a duvet and the tissues because I know she'll need them.

Mum curls up on the sofa with her plate of pie and peas. I slip beneath the duvet and lean into her. The images flicker on the screen, but I'm not watching. Anyway, I've seen the film a million times before. I'm thinking about tomorrow. I tick off the checklist in my head: kitchen cleaned, toilets

Scarlet Ibis

bleached, clothes washed, beds changed, fish fingers and chips in the freezer for supper. I've even left my own room untidy so Mrs Gideon thinks I'm the messy one and Mum has done all the hard work. I've hidden Red's feathers beneath the bed too. I don't want anything to happen that could mess things up again. We've used up our last chances and the Penguin's got her beady eye on us.

I take Mum's empty plate, wash it in the sink, and leave it on the rack to dry. When I go back to Mum, the *Titanic* song is playing. The actors are standing on the prow of the ship, their arms outstretched like birds' wings. Mum's mouthing her favourite line of the song and her face is wet with tears. She's staring at the photo in the silver frame in her hands. I pass her the tissues, curl up next to her, and look at the only picture she has of my dad. He's smiling into the camera. Behind him, scarlet ibis are scattered against a sunset sky. That's how I got my name. Scarlet Ibis Mackenzie. Scarlet Ibis, from the bright red birds that live in the Caroni Swamp below the blue mountains of the Northern Range in Trinidad. That's where my dad's from. Trinidad. Mum says one day he'll come back and find us and take us out there. Her and Red and me.

I stare at the photo of my dad. He's looking at the camera, as if he's looking right at me. Mum says I have his eyes and smile. She says I have his skin too. *Like the colour of soft caramel.* When I was little she used to say she could eat me up. But I've never seen my dad. Except in that photo. I've never seen Red's daddy either. Red's hair is a shock of orange and his skin's like Mum's. It's white, white, white. We don't look much like brother and sister. Sometimes I reckon that might even be part of the problem. Maybe if we looked a little bit like each other it might help. Maybe then we could stay together. Maybe then, no one would try to tear us apart.

CHAPTER 2

'Scarlet . . . wake up!'

I feel my duvet being tugged away from me, so I hold on tight and bury my head deeper in my pillow.

'Scarlet!'

I open my eyes and try to blink the sleep away. The digital clock flashes 6.15 a.m. 'Go back to sleep, Red.' I say. 'Too early.'

Red pulls my duvet away. He's jigging on the spot. He can't keep still. 'The egg! It's happening, Scarlet. Come on!'

I wrap my duvet around me and follow him into his room. Outside, a pale grey dawn is bringing colour back across the rooftops. A sliver of golden light between the clouds promises the sun.

Red is crouched beside the window, his face pressed against the glass. 'Look, Scarlet!'

I kneel down beside him and look into the tangle of sticks and plastic. The mother pigeon is nowhere to be seen, but the small white egg has split in half. I can see the chick inside, curled up, folded and squashed inside the shell. It's straining to get out.

'It's stuck, Scarlet.' Red opens the window until it locks on the safety catch and tries to reach his arm through the small gap. 'It needs help.'

I pull Red back. 'It'll be fine, Red. It has to do this for itself.' I wrap my duvet around Red, too, and we sit and watch the small chick fight its way into the world. 'See?' I say, hugging him tight against me. 'The struggle makes him stronger. Sometimes it's ones like him that become the highest flyers.'

The chick doesn't look like a pigeon. It looks prehistoric, a strange mix of duck and dinosaur, with pinkish-grey skin, stubby un-feathered wings, and a large beak. It sits back on its legs, its mouth gaping open, wanting food. Even now, a minute old, it seems hard to believe it could have fitted into the small shell. Wet orange feathers are matted down against its head and body, but as the sun breaks through the clouds the feathers dry into an orange fuzz of fluff.

Scarlet Ibis

I smile and poke Red in the ribs. 'Know who it reminds me of?'

Red frowns. 'Who?'

'You,' I say.

Red leans closer to the window, his face serious. 'You think so?'

'I think so,' I say. 'We'll have to call him Red as well.'

Red studies the chick as it tries to flap its stubby wings. 'But I'm Red,' he says. He points to the chick. 'He's Little Red.'

My alarm clock blares from my bedroom. 'Time to move,' I say. 'Get ready for school.'

Red scowls. 'Not today.'

'Little Red will be fine until you get home. See . . . the mother pigeon's coming back to feed him.'

The mother pigeon lands in a flurry of feathers and she struts along the ledge, inspecting her chick and pulling sticks into place around it. Red watches the chick push its beak into her mouth and drink a pale watery liquid brought up from her stomach. It looks gross, but Red is fascinated.

'Come on, Red,' I say. 'Time to get dressed.'

'He might fall,' says Red.

The nest is wedged in the corner of the window ledge, a

small hop away from the edge. 'Pigeons have been nesting on buildings and cliffs for years,' I say. 'He'll be fine.'

I help Red with his buttons and his socks and then check on Mum. She's fast asleep, her curtains closed. The room smells stale with smoke, so I open the windows to let a little fresh air inside. The ashtray on her bedside table is now full of stubs. It was empty when I went to bed. I write a note and leave it by her bed: *Mrs Gideon coming at 2 p.m. today. Love you, S & R xxx*

I just hope she's awake in time to read it.

I can't concentrate in class. It's the last lesson of the day: geography with Mr Barnes. Or more like geography with Amar and Chalkie, as they're mucking about, flicking paper up the front. Mr Barnes has got no control. Our Year Seven class is known in the staffroom as the Nightmare Class, something Amar and Chalkie claim as their personal achievement.

But I'm not thinking about geography, or Amar and Chalkie. I'm thinking about Mum, knowing that Mrs Gideon is there in our house, right now. I wish I'd had time to buy some more food for the fridge. There's nothing in it now. Mum had eaten the rest of the bread in the night,

Scarlet Ibis

so I had to buy Red a bacon butty from the station for his breakfast. I've got less than a tenner left until Mum gets her benefits next week, and I don't want to break into zoo money. I promised Red we'd go on Sunday.

Amar and Chalkie and the rest of the class are out of their seats and surging through the door before the bell even stops ringing. Mr Barnes looks like he's just survived a tsunami; stunned and relieved he's made it through another lesson. I squeeze out with the others, shoulder my bag, and run along the back streets to Red's school. It's faster than taking the bus in Friday traffic. I want to avoid Sita and her mum too. I don't want them poking their noses into our problems.

Red's in the hall in afterschool care. The other kids are kicking softballs around, but Red is sitting on his own, as usual. His learning support assistant only comes into school in the mornings. Red's by the window, moving his hands and making shadow patterns on the floor. I stand behind him and watch his shadow bird stretch its wings out wide and fly. It soars, wild and free across the strip of sunlight. It's like the part of him no one else can see, except for me.

'Red?' I say.

He snatches his hands away and spins around, his frown tight across his face. The shadow bird has gone.

'Come on, Red. Let's get home.'

Mrs Evans, the school cleaner stops us on the way out. I think she must live at the school. She does a bit of everything; dinner lady, lollipop lady, cleaner. She's always here.

She leans on her mop. 'Glad I caught you, Scarlet.' She looks around, checking no one else can overhear her. 'Ray's on early shift on the zoo gates on Sunday,' she says. 'Get there before ten if you can.'

I smile and nod. Mrs Evans has had a soft spot for Red since he started at the school. She'd seen Red's fascination with birds and the way they followed him around the playground. She'd convinced her husband to sneak us in the zoo for free and he's been doing it ever since. Once a month, Ray lets us in. Mrs Evans reaches down and ruffles Red's hair. 'Good day, Red?'

Red hides his face in my coat and presses against me.

'He's fine,' I say.

'You're in your own world, aren't you Red?' she says. 'Best place I reckon.'

I take Red's hand. 'We'd better go,' I say. 'Thank you. Tell Ray we'll be there early.'

We stop in the express supermarket on the way home and I buy cheese and bread and some broken biscuits from the reduced-to-clear bin. I've got £5.60 left, which has to

Scarlet Ibis

last us the whole weekend. Red wants to buy some birdseed for the mother pigeon, but it's too expensive and I tell him we'll have to give it crusts of bread instead. I take Red's bag as we walk up the stairwell to our flat. I wonder what the Penguin has put in her assessment. I've kept my fingers crossed all day that Mum will be OK.

I push the door to our flat and frown because it's on the catch. My heart starts thumping in my chest. Mum usually keeps the door locked.

I push the door open wider. 'Mum?'

'Scarlet!' Mrs Gideon turns to face me, a smile pulled across her face. She even looks like a penguin with her black trouser suit and great big beaky nose.

I look beyond her to Mum, sitting at the table. Mum is wearing her green shirt and jeans. Her hair's pulled back in a neat ponytail. I think she might even have some make-up on.

Mrs Gideon beams at Red, too. 'I was a bit late today, but at least this way I get to see all of you.'

Red keeps his eyes on the floor and leans into me. I give him a nudge. 'Why don't you put your bag in your room.'

I put the shopping on the table and glance between Mum and Mrs Gideon.

Mum smiles. 'I've been showing Mrs Gideon your school report, telling her what a clever girl you are.'

I glance across at the Penguin. She's got one up on me already, using Mum to snoop into my school reports.

'You're a hard worker,' says Mrs Gideon. She leans forward and winks. 'Maybe you could put a bit of that effort into keeping your room tidy. Your mum could do with a bit of help around the flat.'

I drop my eyes and smile. 'I'll try,' I say, but I want to jump up and punch the air. I've managed to fool the old Penguin, this time at least.

When Mrs Gideon leaves, I shut the door behind her and slide the chain across. It feels like our flat's been holding its breath, waiting for her to go. I rest my head against the door and feel the relief flood from me, too.

Mum pulls a pack of cigarettes from the back pocket of her jeans.

I put the kettle on and sit down next to her. 'What did she say?'

Mum taps the cigarette packet on the table. 'The usual. She asked a lot of questions.'

'What sort?'

'All sorts,' says Mum. ''Specially about Red. She wanted to know all about Red.'

I feel my mouth go dry. 'Red's fine,' I say. 'Just fine. You told her that, didn't you? You told her Red is fine?'

Scarlet Ibis

Mum takes a cigarette and twirls it in her fingers. 'She wanted to know all about the feathers again.'

'You didn't tell her, did you?'

Mum scowls at me. 'Course I did. I even showed her them. Red had put them under his bed.'

I jump up and fling the chair back.

'Scarlet!'

But I don't listen. I'm already running down the hall to Red's room.

'Red?' I whisper.

Red's sitting on his bed, his head clutched in his arms. He's rocking backwards and forwards, backwards and forwards. The wooden feather box lies open on the floor, the feathers scattered as if some strange exotic bird has been savaged in his room. Red hates anyone but me touching his feathers.

I sit next to him on the bed and put my hand on his back. 'Red, it's me, Scarlet.'

Red's blocked me out. He's blocked out the entire world. I pick up the magpie feather, the one we found the other day. I try to press it in his hand.

'Red, feel this one,' I say. 'It's the magpie feather. Feel it.'

Red rocks faster but clutches the feather in his hand.

'Look at it, Red,' I say. 'Look at it.'

But his eyes are tight, tight shut and he draws his arms further around his head.

I start laying the feathers out on the floor, naming them as I put them in order. 'Blackbird, blue tit, guinea fowl, herring gull, house sparrow, lilac-breasted roller, mallard, ostrich, rock dove . . . '

I keep going, the birds' names coming out in a steady rhythm in my voice. Out of the corner of my eye, I see Red stop rocking and slowly uncurl. He slides down beside me and watches.

' . . . song thrush, tanager . . . '

Red picks up a small green feather and places it down between the soft ostrich feather and the silvery rock dove feather. 'Ring-necked parakeet,' he says.

I smile, and we take turns to place the feathers out in front of us in a long row.

They're in order now, on the floor and in his mind. He counts them all again, mouthing their names, fixing them inside his head.

'We'll find some more on Sunday,' I say.

'A scarlet ibis feather?' asks Red. His eyes are wide, wide open.

I ruffle his hair. 'Let's hope so. We'll just have to see.'

Scarlet Ibis

*

'Fish fingers and chips for tea,' I say.

Mum nods, but she's staring out across the houses. Ash drifts down from her cigarette end to the floor. She doesn't even seem to notice.

I open the window to let the smoke from the room. The safety catch only lets it open a hand's width. I wish we could throw the windows open wide, but we can't, not after what happened last summer. That's when the penguins got involved.

I slide the fish fingers and the chips onto a baking tray and put them in the oven. I'm laying the table when I hear the knock at the door.

'I'll get it,' I yell to Mum.

I put my hand up to the catch, making sure the chain is across. You can't be too careful. Not many people come up here.

I open the door a crack and peer out. Sita and her mum are standing outside.

Sita's mum smiles and holds up something wrapped in brown paper. She's out of her checkout uniform and wearing a long green sari. Swirls of gold run through the material. 'We've brought you some banana cake,' she says.

I take the chain off the catch and stick my head out to see if they are with anyone, but they're on their own.

Sita's mum pushes the cake into my hands. 'Is everything OK, Scarlet?' she asks. 'I met Mrs Gideon on the stairs earlier.'

I look at her, and then at Sita. Sita smiles and stares down at the floor. Sita and I used to be friends. Best friends. But that was before last summer. I know it was Sita who told her mum about Red climbing out on the window ledge of our flat, dressed in the wings we'd made for him. I know it was Sita's mum who had called the penguins and told them all about my mum, too. That's why they took Red and me away the first time.

'Everything's fine,' I say.

Sita's mum takes a step closer. 'Sure?'

'Sure,' I say. I glance back to the kitchen. 'I have to go. Tea's ready.' I start shutting the door. 'Thank you for the cake.'

I push the door and hear the click. I slide the chain across and deadlock the door. I won't ever let them in again. This is our place. The world can spin and spin and spin around us, but we're safe up here.

Mum and Red and me.

We're just fine, the three of us.

And I won't let anyone ever change that again.

CHAPTER 3

There's another storm coming. Red can feel it. He senses it long before I do.

At first Mum goes quiet. Her mood is like a dark cloud, spreading across the flat. It unfurls and makes everything seem heavy and still, like the sky is pressing down on us. When the storm breaks, Mum lashes out. She targets Red. She yells at him. She tells him stuff I know she doesn't mean. Red stays away from her. It's me he looks for. Some nights he creeps in bed with me. I tell him that deep down Mum loves him, but I don't think he believes me, not after some of the things she's said to him.

Mum sinks so deep into herself. She wraps herself in layers and goes somewhere I can't reach her. All I can do is wait. Wait for the storm to pass. It might take days, or even weeks. But I know she's in there, and I know she doesn't want it to be this way.

It's just the way it is.

So, I keep our world together, keep the flat tidy, put food on the table, and look after Red. And all I can do is hope; hope she can find her way back to us again.

The sun streams through the window, glaring off the kitchen table. I give a deep sigh and finish making sandwiches. Red reaches across and takes a slice of bread.

'Don't, Red,' I say. 'I have to save some for tomorrow.'

'It's not for me,' he says. He grabs my hand. 'Come and see,'

I let him pull me to his bedroom. The curtains are still closed, but I can hear a tap-tap-tapping on the window.

'Look,' says Red. He pulls back the curtain.

I crouch down beside him. Outside, the mother pigeon is looking in at us, her head tipped to one side. She's not afraid of us at all. She lifts her beak and taps again at the window.

A sly grin spreads across Red's face. 'I've been feeding her all week.'

'Red!'

'She's hungry, too,' says Red.

Scarlet Ibis

I watch him crumble the piece of bread and drop it through the small gap in the open window. The mother pigeon pecks at the fallen crumbs on the narrow ledge and taps on the window again for more.

It's been almost a week since Little Red hatched from his shell. In that time we've watched him fill out and grow. He's doubled in size. Stubs of adult feathers show beneath his fuzz of orange fluff. Some mornings frost-patterns have crept across the windows, but I imagine he must be warm, protected beneath his mother's soft feathers.

I stand up and stretch my legs. 'Once you've fed her, get your coat, Red. It'll be cold out there.' I lean forward and whisper, 'it's zoo day.'

'Zoo day,' Red repeats. He knows it's zoo day. He's been up since six, watching the hands on his clock turn slowly round to nine o'clock.

I grab my bag, pack a book, our lunch, and the envelope of zoo money I'd hidden away.

'Come on,' says Red. He's already by the door, jigging on the spot.

I pull his coat straight and help him with his boots.

'Bye Mum,' I yell. 'We're going out.'

Mum's in the sitting room, on the sofa. The TV's blaring, but she's not watching it. She's staring into space.

'I've put some sandwiches in the fridge for you,' I say. 'Cheese and mayo.'

Mum doesn't say anything.

I walk up and crouch down beside her. 'We'll be back this afternoon.'

Mum lights a cigarette and draws on it deeply. She breathes out, filling the space between us with grey smoke. 'OK,' she says. She doesn't even look at me.

I follow Red out of the flat, and glance once at Mum before I shut the door behind us. She's sitting perfectly still, as if time has stopped around her. Only the slowly rising spiral of cigarette smoke gives it away. I hate thinking of Mum alone like this. I wish I really could stop time in our flat and keep her safe until we return.

Outside the sky is pale blue. I breathe in deeply. The air is clear and sharp. It's the first sunny day we've had this April. Red knows the way to the zoo off by heart. I follow him down the High Street, past people sitting at tables outside cafes, drinking coffee and eating Sunday breakfasts. They're wrapped up in coats and hats, but sitting in the sun. Everyone is smiling today. Sunshine happy people. I wish the sun shone every day.

We're early at the zoo, and have to wait for quarter of an hour before we're let in. I count out the money I've saved

Scarlet Ibis

over the month. Mum doesn't know I put aside some of the food money she gives to me. I try to save enough for chips and an ice cream at the zoo for Red and me. It's our special treat. Our little ritual. I keep the money in an envelope hidden beneath the carpet in my room. I feel guilty about not telling Mum, but the zoo is Red's special place. It keeps him going, knowing we'll visit on the last Sunday of every month.

I'm glad that Ray is on duty early at the gate. Red likes being the first ones in, the first to see the animals that day. I tell him we're like explorers, seeing the animals for the very first time. He likes to see them in peace and quiet too, without hordes of other people crowding round him.

There are only four ticket booths open at this time of day. I see Ray through the glass of booth number four, his bulk almost filling up his small cubicle. I keep my hood up, stand up tall, and hope no one suspects I'm not sixteen. We're not allowed in without an adult. It's not as if Mum would ever bring us here. We couldn't afford it anyway. The price of a family ticket would keep us in food for at least two weeks.

'Two tickets please,' I say.

Ray goes through the motions, pretending to exchange money. I know he's risking his job, letting us in for free. I'd hate it if he got found out because of me.

He grins. 'Enjoy your day.'

I want to thank him, but Red is already pulling me into the zoo.

'Where shall we go first?' I say.

Red points towards the underpass. 'Africa!'

I let him run ahead. I know where he's going. We always have to go the same way around the zoo, starting at the African mammals. We walk through Nightlife and try to spot the bush babies leaping in the darkness. We pass the lemurs and the otters, and walk beneath the underpass again until we reach Penguin Beach.

It's almost feeding time and the penguins are lined up on the small stretch of beach, waiting. A rock-hopper penguin waddles towards us, yabbering away, as penguins like to do.

I nudge Red. 'Mrs Gideon is coming to get you.'

Red squeals and runs away.

'Hey, Red, come back. It's feeding time soon.'

Red shakes his head and points beyond the pelicans, along the maze of shrub-lined pathways. 'Scarlet ibis,' he shouts.

We usually save the birds of the Blackburn Pavilion until last, but Red seems in a hurry. He's fixed his mind on finding a scarlet ibis feather today. He doesn't even have

Scarlet Ibis

time to stop and watch the mechanical birds fly around the Hunkin Clock.

We leave a cold April London and step into the tropics. Rainforest surrounds us. Sunlight streams through the glass roof and filters down through the canopy of leaves. The air is warm and humid. It clings to my clothes and skin. Birdsong and the sound of rushing water fills the space around us. High above, small birds flit over our heads, their colours electric in the sunshine. I always wonder if they know that there's a whole world beyond those windows where some birds are flying freely. Maybe they can't imagine life another way. Maybe it would be too hard if they could. Lower down, the larger birds, the red-crested turacos and the fruit doves, hop between the branches. On the dappled sunlit floor, black-necked stilts and other ground birds scurry in search of food. I sit down on one of the wooden benches by the exit. 'I'll wait here,' I say.

Red nods and I watch him walk away. His eyes are scanning the aviary for all the birds he wants to see. He'll look for them among the leaves and branches, hidden behind tall grasses or tucked away in roost boxes. He won't go until he's spied every one and counted them on his fingers; the black-naped fruit dove, the hooded pitta, the red-whiskered bulbul, the orange-headed thrush, and the bleeding heart doves that remind me so much of Mum. Red sits crossed-legged in a patch of sunlight, just watching and counting, silently mouthing the names of birds.

I take out my book, a new one from the library. Red can watch the birds for hours. They calm him and pull his thoughts together. They make him feel safe inside. It's the only time he sits still, without fidgeting, or rocking, or jiggling his legs. With Red absorbed, it's the only time I ever find to read, the only time I can live in worlds other than my own. The zoo is Red's refuge. Books are mine.

I'm on chapter five when Red sits down beside me. 'Are you done?' I say.

Red nods. He holds up a tiny feather; it shines electric blue in the sunlight. 'Splendid sunbird,' he says. A big grin is stretched across his face.

It's one he hasn't got. I take it from him and slide it into the zipper section of my bag. 'Come on,' I say. 'Let's see the scarlet ibis and then have lunch.' I close my book, imagining the characters frozen in their own time until I open the pages and start reading again. I wonder if our own lives are written down, unchangeable. I wonder what would be written down for me.

We leave the heat of the jungle and I follow Red through the foyer of the Blackburn Pavilion to the aviaries outside. I

Scarlet Ibis

pull my jacket around me and turn to look through the cage wire for the scarlet ibis. We see them standing on a mound of earth, beyond a pool of still green water, their feathers fluffed and beaks tucked beneath their wings. They're shut out from their indoor enclosure. They must be freezing too.

'They're too cold to move,' I say.

Red presses his nose against the wire. These are his favourite birds. He points up into a small tree. Sunlight catches a lone scarlet ibis perched on a branch. Its feathers range from flame-orange to deep scarlet, and its head is turned so that its long curved bill rests on its body. Bright pink legs end in long toes that curl around the branch. It's hard to believe anything in nature can be so red.

I look down to smile at Red, but he's not looking at the bird any more. His eyes are fixed on the pool of green water. In the middle, slowly turning in the breeze, floats a single feather. It's a long flight feather, bright scarlet and tipped with black.

'There,' he says.

I look at the feather, the one that Red has been dreaming about all week. 'I can't reach it, Red.'

But Red has other ideas. He pulls me away and back into the foyer of the pavilion. He points at a door next to the scarlet ibis enclosure. *No Entry. Staff Only.*

I look around me. The zoo is busy now. There's no way we could get in there without being seen.

'We can't, Red. It'll be locked, anyway.'

Red turns the handle and pushes the door open just a crack. He turns to me, wide-eyed.

Before I can stop him, Red slips through.

'Red,' I hiss, but the door closes shut behind him.

I look around me. No one has even noticed us, so I follow Red and find myself standing on the wet concrete floor of the scarlet ibis indoor enclosure. The place smells damp and vaguely fishy. A strip light flickers on the ceiling. Red has already crossed to the far side and opened the door to the outdoor aviary.

I can see through to the green pond and the feather twirling on its surface.

'Red, no . . . '

But Red can't wait. He walks into the sunlight. I stay hidden inside, but I can see Red standing at the pond edge, staring at the feather. It almost glows against the dark green water. People are looking and pointing at him from the other side of the aviary, but he doesn't notice them at all.

Maybe I can rush in and grab it for him. I look at the water and floating scum. The pond doesn't look deep, but I bet the bottom is covered in slime.

Red crouches down and leans out across the water, trying to reach the feather. He stretches far out, too far.

'Red,' I yell.

But it's too late.

His foot slips and he plunges forwards into the pool. I watch as his head goes right under.

'HEY! HEY YOU!'

I look up and see one of the zookeepers. He flings his bucket down, scattering seed and fruit across the ground, and starts running towards us. My heart is thumping inside my chest, because I know that we are now in deep, deep trouble.

CHAPTER 4

The keeper wades into the pool and hauls Red from the water. Red's soaking and covered in green sludge. Water has filled his nose and mouth. He's coughing and spluttering and trying to scrape the slime from his face.

The keeper lifts Red onto the concrete and holds him by his coat.

'Let him go,' I yell. Red hates being held by anyone but me. I know he'll panic.

Red can feel the man's hands. He starts wriggling and clawing at him.

'Let him go!'

Red shrieks and snorts and twists. He sounds more like a trapped animal than a boy. He sinks his teeth into the keeper's hand. The keeper lets go, and I crouch down

Scarlet Ibis

beside Red and put my arms around him, but he's lost inside himself and he's fighting me now too. One of Red's hands comes free and cracks me on the nose. I hear the keeper speak into his walkie-talkie. It buzzes and crackles and I can hear another voice.

Red's yells are getting louder. He's on his side, flinging his arms around, kicking his legs against the ground. People are watching us, staring in at us. We're part of the entertainment now.

I try to hold him. 'Red, it's me. It's me, Scarlet.'

But Red can't hear me. He's lost inside himself.

The keeper crouches down beside me and tries to hold Red's head to stop him banging it against the ground. He looks around him then turns to me. 'Where's his mum or dad? Who's looking after him?'

'I am,' I say. 'I'm his sister.'

I see him look between us, taking us both in. Working it out.

The keeper frowns. 'Are you on your own?'

If he finds out we got in the zoo by ourselves, Ray will get in big, big trouble. 'Mum had to take our little sister home 'cos she was sick,' I lie. 'She's coming back for us in a while.'

The keeper is distracted by Red's cries.

I can hardly hold Red still.

The keeper takes off his jacket and pushes it beneath Red's head. 'Is he on tablets? Medication? What does he need?'

'He needs the feather,' I say.

The keeper frowns. 'The feather?'

I nod my head in the direction of the pond. 'He wants that one. The scarlet ibis feather.'

The keeper looks at Red, then wades across the pond and returns with the feather.

'Red,' I say. 'I've got it.' Red's hands are balled up in fists. Blood is running from the corner of his mouth. He must have bitten his tongue. I try to slide the feather shaft into his closed hand. 'Look, Red. It's the scarlet ibis feather. The one you wanted.'

Red opens one eye and peers at the feather. His body's trembling, but the feather holds him. It's a long flight feather. The barbs are straggly and wet, but I smooth them, bringing them together, making the feather perfect. Making it whole again. I feel Red slowly relax. He opens the other eye and just stares at the feather.

'See?' I smile at him and stroke his forehead. 'We got it, didn't we?'

When I look up, another zoo keeper has joined us. She's young, her blonde hair is scraped back from her face. She kneels down and looks at Red. 'You OK, mate?'

Scarlet Ibis

'He'll be fine,' I say.

She stands up and brushes her trousers. She looks around at the crowd staring in. 'Reckon we need to get you out of here and cleaned up a bit.'

I help Red to his feet. 'I'll take him home.'

The keeper shakes her head. 'He'll freeze in those wet things. We've got some spare overalls in the Prep Room. He can wear those while we dry his clothes.'

I look at Red. His teeth are chattering and he's beginning to shiver. He needs to get dry. I know we shouldn't go off with strangers, but I don't know what else to do. 'Where's the Prep Room?'

She nods her head across to the other side of the zoo. 'Not far.'

I take Red by the arm and follow the keepers out of the pavilion and across the zoo. The wind bites at my skin, and I can see Red's lips and hands are blue.

The keeper opens the door of the Prep Room and smiles. 'I'm Amy, by the way. Reptile Woman.' She points at the keeper who first found us. 'And this is Jim. He's in charge of the birds. He's the Birdman.'

Jim gives a thumbs-up. 'Do you want us to call your mum?'

I shake my head. 'Home's not far. We'll be OK.'

*

The Prep Room is clean and dry, and it's warm in here too. Boxes of fruits and nuts are stacked against the wall. Chopping boards and knives lie on the work surfaces, and a pile of clean overalls and towels are folded on top of a washing machine.

Amy holds up some overalls. 'They're a bit big, but we can roll up the sleeves and trouser legs.'

I help Red take off his wet clothes and climb into the overalls. Red won't let go of the feather. He holds it in his hand as I slide his arms through the sleeves.

Amy rolls up the wet clothes to take them away to dry. She holds up Red's coat and tries to scrape off the slime clinging to the back, cuffs, and sleeves. 'I'll try to get most of it off,' she says, 'but it'll need a good wash when you get home. Hope your mum won't mind.'

'It's fine,' I say.

Amy puts the coat over a radiator to dry. 'It's what mums are for, eh?'

I smile, but stare at the floor.

Amy empties the muddy water from Red's trainers into the sink and passes me some huge boots for Red to borrow.

Scarlet Ibis

I hold them up for Red. 'What d'you think, Red?'

But he's crouching down beside a wire basket on the floor, staring at a grey ball of fluffy feathers inside.

'That's Woody,' says Jim. He's a wood owl.'

Amy elbows Jim in the ribs. 'Really original! Must've taken you an age to think that name up.'

Jim kneels down beside Red. 'He's only young, but his mum rejected him. We've got to feed him now.'

Red presses his face closer to the basket.

'I'll get him out,' says Jim. 'His feed's due about now. You can help if you like.'

I watch as Red sits cross legged while Jim places the owl chick on his lap. Red wraps his hands around the soft feathers. He's never held a bird before. Woody's heart-shaped face stares up, his huge black eyes fixed on Red's.

'He likes *you*,' says Jim.

Red smiles. He runs his finger from the top of Woody's head to his stump of a tail. Woody opens his beak so wide I can see right down his throat.

'You'd better feed him,' says Jim. 'It might not look very nice but his dinner's chopped up day-old chicks.'

I feel a bit sick seeing the bits of heads and legs all jumbled up together, but Red doesn't seem to mind. He picks up a piece and dangles it in front of Woody.

'Bit closer,' says Jim.

Red lowers his hand and Woody snatches the piece of chick, swallowing it down with huge gulps.

'Well done,' says Jim. 'He wouldn't take it from me this morning. Keep going.'

We watch Red feed Woody. Red's forehead is knotted in concentration. It's as if the owl chick is the only thing that exists in his world.

Amy smiles. 'Hey Jim, I reckon you've found yourself a soulmate there.'

Jim puts his hand on Red's shoulder. 'We have ourselves another birdman.'

Red looks up, right at Jim. He looks him right in the eye. A small smile curls at the corners of his mouth. 'I'm Bird Boy,' he says.

I miss a breath.

Red never looks directly at anyone, never speaks to them, or smiles. The doctors say it's part of his condition. The only person to ever see him smile is me.

'Bird Boy,' says Jim. He watches Red feed another piece of meat to Woody, and doesn't even realize the miracle he's done.

It's one small moment, one fleeting moment, but for me the world has tilted on its axis and thrown us on a different course.

Scarlet Ibis

Maybe the doctors are wrong about Red. Maybe there is a key to his condition. Maybe we've just found it and can help him.

My stomach growls really loudly and Jim checks his watch. 'Woody's had his lunch. I guess it's our turn now.'

'Come on,' says Amy, 'I'll take you both to the cafe while the clothes are drying. I'm sure Sandra will find you something to eat.'

Red follows Amy out through the door. He's clutching the scarlet ibis feather in one hand, stroking it with the other. I turn back to Jim. 'Thank you for the feather.'

'That's OK,' he says. He puts Woody back in the wire basket. 'What's with the feather thing, anyway?'

I shrug my shoulders. 'He collects them.'

Jim washes his hands and shakes them dry. 'Well, I guess there's no harm in that.' He smiles. 'Unless of course you go drowning yourself in the process.'

I pick at the frayed edges of my coat. 'Red's different,' I say. I don't usually talk to people about Red. The doctors have given him their labels. He doesn't need any more. But Jim's the Birdman, and Red seems to trust him. 'Red needs the feathers. They're like the missing pieces of himself he's trying to find. He needs them to find his way into our world.'

Jim looks ahead at Red and smiles. 'Maybe he needs them to help him fly.'

I smile back, because I think Jim is the first person I've met who actually understands.

I tell Red to eat as much as he can, because we don't have to pay for any of it. Sandra has let us choose anything we want from the cafe. I take a huge plate of curry, rice and salad, and a massive slice of cake and an apple. Red has a burger with loads of chips that he covers in tomato sauce. Sandra brings us two mugs of hot chocolate with cream and marshmallows.

I feel so full afterwards that I don't think I can move. Even Red flops back in his chair. I lean across to him and whisper, 'whatever you do, Red, don't be sick. You don't want to waste a meal like this!'

We wait there, in the warm fug of the cafe, until Amy comes to find us. 'How're you guys doing? Do you want anything else to eat?'

'Couldn't fit it in,' I say.

'Well, Jim's got your clothes ready. He's found something else for you, too.'

Scarlet Ibis

Back in the Prep Room, I help Red into his clothes. They still smell pretty bad, but at least they're dry. His trainers are damp, but they'll be OK until we get home.

'Here,' says Jim. 'You might like these.' He hands Red a plastic bag.

Red looks inside and his eyes widen. He turns to me and shows me what's inside.

Feathers. A bag full of feathers. All colours and sizes. Flight feathers, downy feathers, display feathers.

'I always pick up the nice ones,' says Jim. 'Don't know why. They're too good to leave lying around.'

Red pulls out a long blue feather, half the length of his arm.

'Hyacinth macaw,' he says. He pulls out another. It's long and feathery, dark blue-grey. 'Cassowary.' He pulls out feather after feather . . . 'Socorro dove, blue-winged kookaburra, white pelican . . . '

Jim laughs. 'You know them all. I reckon you should get home before you put me out of a job.'

I get up to leave. 'We'd better go.'

Jim smiles. 'Well, come back again and see us,' he says. 'I'll look out for more feathers.'

I walk with Red towards the exit. Red's buzzing. He's reeling off the names of the feathers in the bag. He can't stop talking. The sky is clear and blue. Although the air is cold, I can feel the sun's warm rays deep beneath my skin. It's been the perfect day. An amazing day. Miracles have happened. I've never seen Red like this. Maybe sunshine can make *everyone* happy.

Then I see it in the gift shop window. It's a Sun Jar. It looks just like an old-fashioned jam jar, but tiny solar lights inside collect sunlight and give out a warm golden glow at night.

I feel for the zoo money in my pocket. We didn't buy chips and ice cream, so I've got just about enough.

I have to get it.

It's the perfect thing for Mum.

Maybe I can make her happy, if I can bring back home the sun.

CHAPTER 5

'How much was it?' Mum holds the Sun Jar right in my face. It glows with a faint golden light.

'It was half price,' I say.

Mum slams it down on the table. 'It's useless. What's the point in it?'

I stare at the Sun Jar and feel my eyes burn with tears.

Mum sits down and pulls a cigarette from the packet on the table. 'What are we going to eat tonight? There's nothing in the fridge.'

I spill my loose change on the table. 'I've got enough for pasta and a tin of tomatoes,' I say. 'I'll go out now and get some.'

Mum lights up the cigarette, but doesn't take her eyes off me. 'I give you money to buy food, but all you do is waste it on stuff like this.' She swipes the Sun Jar with her hand. It flies off the table and cracks against the wall. The golden glow flickers and dies inside.

The sunlight I brought home has been snuffed out.

Mum leans forward, her face knotted with disgust. 'You and Red can forget the zoo next time, too.'

I feel blood rush to my head. I grab the pack of cigarettes and crush it in my hand. I hold it in her face and scream at her. 'All *you* do is spend it on this.'

Mum slumps back and stares at me. Silence fills the space between us. I never shout at Mum. I usually tread around her, as if I'm walking across shards of broken glass. I don't know what she'll do now. I feel sick and dizzy, and hold onto the edges of the table.

Mum flicks ash into an empty mug. Her mouth is a thin hard line. 'Get out,' she says. She speaks the words so quietly, but I hear every word. 'You stupid girl. Get out of my sight.'

I drop the crushed packet on the table and run to my room. I lie in bed and pull the covers right up over me. I curl up in a ball and close my eyes so tight it hurts. Mum's right. I am stupid. Useless. I can't do anything. I can't do anything at all.

I can't make her love me.

I can't even make her smile.

I feel Red creep into bed with me. He's clutching the scarlet ibis feather in his hand. He squirms his way in and lies with his back to me. I wrap my arms around him and rest my head against his.

'Tell me a story,' he says.

'Forget it, Red,' I say. 'Not tonight.'

'Caroni Swamp?'

'Just leave it,' I snap.

Red threads his fingers into mine. 'Some day,' he begins, 'we'll find ourselves an aeroplane, and fly up into the big blue sky.'

I hug Red tight against me.

'You tell it, Scarlet,' he says. 'You always tell it better than me.'

I bury my head in his back. 'And we'll be like birds, the two of us,' I say. 'Just us.' Hot tears slide down my face and soak into the cotton of his pyjamas. 'We'll fly above the streets and houses, above Big Ben and The Eye and London Zoo. We'll fly across the whole Atlantic Ocean, all the way to Trinidad.' I tell the story. I tell it for Red, just how I always do, but this time I don't believe it. Like the Sun Jar, I feel as if a light inside me has gone out, and it's become too cold and dark to feel anything at all.

CHAPTER 6

Red wakes up in the morning with a fever. He's hot and sweating. I wonder if he swallowed some dirty water from the pool at the zoo. I daren't tell Mum about it.

I fetch some paracetamol from the bathroom and give him half a tablet. 'Do you want some toast?'

Red nods and lies back in bed. There's no way he can go to school today. I pass Mum's bedroom. The lights are out and the curtains are drawn. She's fast asleep.

I put the kettle on and stick some bread into the toaster. Maybe I should pretend I'm sick today and stay home to look after Red. I wouldn't think twice about it any other day, but a theatre company is coming to school today, and Mrs Pike's picked just me and Sita from our class to join a drama workshop with them after school. I've been looking forward to it all term.

I'd ask Sita's mum to check on Red, but I don't want the Penguins coming back. There's no one else to call.

I jump when the toast pops up. The clock on the oven says quarter to eight. I'll have to make a decision soon.

I search through the cupboard hoping to find a jar of jam I've somehow missed, but there's nothing there, only the empty one I've scraped out for the last few weeks. There's a bit of jam clinging to the inside of the lid. I spread that thinly on the corner of his toast and take it to him with a glass of water on a tray. I'm glad to see him out of bed. He's kneeling beside the window, peering at the chick.

I put the tray on Red's bed and kneel down beside him. A gust of wind smatters rain against the glass. Little Red is hunched low, shivering in the nest, waiting for his mother to return. He looks wet and cold. Water runs down his head and drips off the stubs of flight feathers beginning to grow from the edges of his wings. The feathers are a mixture of rust-red and white, not the storm grey of his mother's.

Red presses his face closer to the glass. 'Can't we keep him in here with us and feed him, like I did with Woody?'

'He's a wild bird,' I say. 'His mother's looking after him.'

'But what if something happens to her? What if she doesn't come back, what then?

'Tell you what,' I say. 'If she doesn't come back, you can be the one to look after him. Do you think you can do that?'

Red nods, his face solemn and serious.

I'm sure the mother will come back, but if I put Red in charge of looking after the chick, then at least he'll have something to do all day. He probably won't move from here until I return.

'I have to go to school now,' I say, 'but you can keep an eye on Little Red *all* day. It's up to you to make sure he's OK.'

Red pulls his beanbag near the window and settles down with his toast to watch Little Red. He looks a bit better already and he wants to eat. Maybe he'll be OK with Mum today. He has all the new feathers from the zoo to keep him busy, too.

I take Mum a plate of toast as well. 'Mum?'

Mum sits up in bed, wiping sleep from her eyes.

'I brought you breakfast.' I put the plate beside her on the bedcover. 'Red's sick today,' I say. 'There's a bug going round his school.'

Mum reaches for her cigarettes.

'He needs a day off,' I say.

Scarlet Ibis

Mum raises an eyebrow. 'So . . . ?'

'Are you OK with him at home?'

'I'm not going anywhere, am I!' she says.

I back out of her room. 'OK,' I say. 'I'll get supper for us on my way home.'

'Scarlet?'

'Yes?'

'I'd love a cup of tea.' She holds a cigarette between her fingers. 'And my lighter. Can you find it for me before you go?'

I feel bad leaving Red, but he's happy watching Little Red, so I don't think he can be all that sick. If he's not right tomorrow, I'll try to get Mum to take him to the doctor's.

At school, I hardly think of Mum and Red all day. The theatre company presents their play to all the Year Sevens. It's is a mash-up of Shakespeare's plays. When we started *A Midsummer Night's Dream* in class, it was boring and hard to read the language. But the actors have made it come alive. Even Chalkie and Amar are listening, which has to be a first. They're both pulled up on stage to help act out a seven-minute version of *Macbeth*. Chalkie plays Macduff, and Amar plays Macbeth; and they fight each other in the final battle. Amar's death throes go on and on. He flings his arms around and froths at the mouth. It's more pantomime than theatre, but he's actually quite good at it; even the actors and teachers can't help laughing.

Then it's the end of school and I'm in the hall, with Sita and loads of kids from other classes, waiting to start the workshop.

The actors teach us about character—how to live in someone else's skin. I'm a warrior, a farm girl, a stowaway, and a Tudor king.

I can live a thousand lives, be anyone I want to be.

I don't have to be myself.

Beneath the mask and costume, I can be free.

I look across at Sita and wonder if we can step out of our own lives and into someone else's. I try to imagine being her, walking into her flat, sitting at the table with her mum and dad and younger brother, eating Mrs Kanwar's lime curry. I can almost imagine I'm there, listening to the chat around the table, Sita's dad helping with homework, her younger brother making model aeroplanes at his desk. I remember playing at Sita's house for hours, especially when Red was born. Mrs Kanwar used to cook us all supper twice a week. She looked after us back then. I don't think Mum could have done without her. Maybe I should have asked Sita's mum to check on Red today.

I sit with Sita on the bus back home. It's the first time I've sat next to her all year. She looks really pleased, and I feel bad for ignoring her before.

She opens a packet of sweets and offers me one. 'You're really good at acting.'

I take a sweet. 'You too.'

Sita shakes her head. 'No, I mean it. Even the actors noticed. You were *really* good.'

I put the sweet in my mouth and smile. 'You think so?'

Sita smiles back. 'I know so.' She pulls an exercise book from her bag. 'We should write some plays, like when we were little.'

'I hope they're better than the ones we used to do,' I say.

Sita starts to giggle. 'Do you remember the one about the donkey and the frog?'

I close my eyes and bang my head against the headrest in front of me. 'Oh no! Not that one!' I start giggling too. 'We played that every day at break time, didn't we?'

'HEE-HAW!' brays Sita, right into my ear.

I almost choke on my sweet, laughing.

'GRIBBIT!' I croak.

'HEE-HAW!'

'GRIBBIT! GRIBBIT! GRIBBIT!'

'HEEEEEEEEEE-HAAAAW!'

We can't stop laughing. People on the bus are turning in their seats to stare at us, but I don't care. Tears are rolling down Sita's face, and I have to hold my sides they hurt so much. Sita's grinning at me and I grin back. I hadn't realized how much I'd missed her.

I slump back in my seat. 'D'you want to come round to mine tonight?'

'Cool,' says Sita, and gives me one of her biggest smiles.

Outside, the traffic has come to a standstill. I crane my neck to see why we've stopped. I don't want to be too late getting home. At the far end of the street, an ambulance fights its way through the cars and lorries, its blue lights flashing. I hate the lights and the sirens. Every time I hear them, they fill me with a sense of dread that doesn't go until I know Mum and Red are OK. Our bus inches forward in the rush hour traffic. Two fire engines blare past us, moving through the red traffic lights as cars and taxis let them pass.

Ahead, I see a cloud of black smoke billowing up into the sky. It's somewhere near the station. Somewhere near our flat. I know I shouldn't worry. London's full of buildings. It could be the station, or any block of flats, not ours.

But it *is* ours.

Scarlet Ibis

*

The bus turns the corner and I see the fire engines pulled up, firing water cannons into the sky. Black smoke hangs in the air. People are massed in small groups in the street, their necks craned upwards. Smoke and flames pour from the windows of the top flat.

Our flat.

I run out of the bus. I look around the people, searching for Mum and Red. Sita runs to her mum and dad and brother. They wrap their arms around her, pulling her close. Mrs Kanwar's uniform is blackened with soot and smoke. She calls out to me. But I'm looking for Mum and Red. I spin round and round and round. But I can't see them at all. They must still be up there, in the flat.

'MUM! RED!' I start running to the stairwell, but the entrance is blocked by two firefighters, so I run to the front of the flats and look up. 'MUM! RED!'

Smoke is pouring from the windows, flames licking up the sides. The plastic window ledge of Red's room has buckled in the heat. Little Red won't have survived this heat. I scan the ground beneath his window and see a tangle of sticks and plastic half hidden in the weed-filled flowerbed. Somehow the nest has survived the fall.

Then I see Little Red, curled inside. His fuzz of feathers is blackened, and he's breathing so hard that his beak is open. But he's alive.

Maybe Red is alive, too.

I scoop up the nest with Red's pigeon and wedge it in my schoolbag, between my files and textbooks. I just have to hope it will be OK in there for now. I shoulder my bag and run back to the stairwell. I try to push my way through.

'My brother's up there,' I yell.

But I feel arms grab me and pull me back. 'Let me go.' I kick and scream at the firefighter holding me. 'Let. Me. Go.'

The firefighter lifts me up and carries me away. 'No one can go in. It's not safe. It's not safe for anyone at all.'

CHAPTER 7

Time passes in a blur. The world spins in a kaleidoscope
of blue lights and different faces. I'm in a fire engine,
a police car, a police station, an ambulance. The world spins
and spins and spins. No one knows what to do with me.
I try to picture Mum and Red in my mind, but I can't see
them at all. I want to wake up from this nightmare.

'Scarlet?'

The voice anchors me to the seat. I'm sitting in a small
hospital room. The pale green walls are hung with canvas
lily prints. A water dispenser gurgles in the corner. The
lighting is low and soft. This is the sort of room where
doctors break bad news.

'Scarlet?' Mrs Gideon sits beside me.

'Where's Red and Mum?'

Mrs Gideon puts her hand on my arm. 'They're both in hospital.'

I take a deep breath and grip the edges of my seat. 'Alive?'

She nods. 'Alive.'

I sink my head onto my chest and close my eyes.

Alive!

My whole body starts to shake and shake. I have to wrap my arms around myself and hold on tight.

I feel Mrs Gideon 's arms around me too.

'A neighbour pulled them from the flat.'

I think of the soot on Mrs Kanwar's uniform. So she saved Mum and Red. She must've kept a key to our flat. Maybe she always knew something like this would happen.

'I need to see Mum and Red,' I say.

Mrs Gideon doesn't say a word. I open my eyes and look at her. She's wearing a jumper and old jeans. Her hair's ruffled, and she doesn't have her satchel of spy-notes. She doesn't look like a penguin today. She looks almost human.

'I need to see them now,' I say.

'They're in intensive care,' she says, 'for smoke inhalation. The doctors are looking after them, and I've found someone to look after you.'

'I want to stay with them. I'm staying right here.'

'They're not at this hospital,' she says.

Scarlet Ibis

I get up. 'Then take me to them,' I shout.

Mrs Gideon shakes her head. 'I can't,' she says. 'I've found you emergency foster care for tonight.'

'I just want Red and Mum,' I say.

Mrs Gideon stands up and takes her keys from her pocket. 'I know,' she says. 'But you need somewhere to go, for now. Somewhere safe while we decide what's best to do.'

What's best to do. The words ring hollow, deep inside. I've heard those words before.

I follow her to her car. Mrs Gideon opens the front passenger door for me, but I don't want to sit anywhere near her, so I get into the backseat and strap myself in. I wait for the barrage of questions, but Mrs Gideon puts some music on instead. Maybe she doesn't feel like talking either.

It's only now that I get to check on Little Red. I open my schoolbag and look inside. The nest is squashed, but it's held together and protected the little chick. When I touch him, he lifts his wobbly head and makes high peeping noises, calling for his mother. But it's only me here now, and I don't have anything to give him. I don't even know if his mother survived. It's not as if I can take him back. He's got no home to go back to either. I'll have to find food for him, somehow. I can't let Red's pigeon die.

I hug the bag to my chest and slump against the window, the pane cold against my cheek. Outside it's dark already. Rain has started to fall in big splotches on the window. I watch the raindrops chase each other in hurried streaks along the glass. I remember the last time Red and I were taken into foster care. Mum had been so ill she'd had to spend a month in hospital. We were placed with Mrs Watts, on the south side of the river. Her house smelt of cats and cat pee, and she had huge plants in every room. She couldn't cope with Red. No one can when he gets really bad. He was taken to another care home, and I didn't see him until we got back home with Mum. I don't think he could have eaten because he'd lost so much weight in that short time.

Mrs Gideon's car crawls through the traffic. Headlights and neon shop signs glare through the window. I don't think we've crossed the river yet. 'I'm not staying with Mrs Watts,' I say.

Mrs Gideon looks at me in the rear-view mirror. 'You're not,' she says. 'I've found a family for you to stay with.'

A family? I don't want other kids around me. I just want Red.

We turn into a cul-de-sac and pull up outside a red-brick semi. Two cars are parked on the paved front garden.

'This is it,' says Mrs Gideon.

Scarlet Ibis

I sink lower in my seat. This is the sort of house I used to dream about, like the ones in adverts on TV where Mum and Red and me would live together. The fridge would always be full and we'd have big parties and friends round every night. We'd have a garden full of flowers and a small scruffy dog called Ronnie with muddy paws. Mum would smile and laugh all day and I'd make cupcakes with her, in a kitchen filled with sunshine. But right now I want to be anywhere but here. Mum and Red aren't here to share the dream.

A hall light comes on and the front door opens, flooding light onto the drive. The woman standing in the doorway isn't white, like Mum or Mrs Watts or Mrs Gideon. She's black, like me.

Mrs Gideon opens the car door. 'This is Renée. She'll be looking after you tonight.'

Renée steps out into the rain and smiles. 'Hi Jo,' she says, and then turns to me. 'You must be Scarlet?'

I nod. I feel small and stupid somehow. All I have is the school uniform I'm wearing, and my school bag. I fold my arm across the bag. I don't want them to see what's inside.

Renée beckons us in. 'Well come on, both of you. Come into the dry.'

We follow her through to the kitchen. It's warm and

clean. Everything matches, from the orange mugs on the mug-stand to the saucepans and cupboard doors. There's even a huge bowl filled with oranges. I glance at the pile of papers on the table. A pen and a mug of half-drunk coffee sit next to it. It looks like a pile of homework. Maybe Renée is a teacher. In the corner of the room, a guitar is propped up against the wall and sheet music is scattered on the floor.

Renée puts the kettle on. 'Would you like a cup of tea, or hot chocolate?'

I shrug my shoulders.

'Well, maybe hot chocolate then.' She spoons heaped teaspoons of hot chocolate powder into a mug. 'It's just me here at the moment. Theo is at work, and Jez is out with friends, so we'll have some peace and quiet for a little while.'

I stare around the room. A black leather double photo frame sits on the work surface. One photo shows a teenage boy playing a guitar, and the other a young woman with braided hair wearing a dark purple prom dress.

Renée sees me looking and picks up the photo frame. 'That's Jez, glued to his guitar as usual. And that's Avril. She's away at uni now, so you can have her room.'

I turn to Mrs Gideon. 'I have to see Mum and Red.'

'Scarlet, we have to let the doctors assess them and take care of them for now.'

Scarlet Ibis

'But I need to see them. Red needs me.'

Renée places the mug and some biscuits on a tray. 'Why don't I show you your room and you can settle in?'

Mrs Gideon smiles. 'That's a good idea.'

I walk upstairs with them, Renée in front and Mrs Gideon behind, as if they're guarding me, preventing my escape. It's not as if I know which hospital Mum and Red are in, anyway. No one tells me anything.

I follow Renée into a small bedroom at the back of the house. Everything is purple: purple walls, purple duvet, and purple carpet. Renée puts the tray on the chest of drawers and turns to me. 'I hope it's OK for you.'

It's not OK. I don't want to be here. I don't have a choice. I place my schoolbag in the corner of the room and hope Little Red doesn't start calling for food. I know they won't want him. I don't want them to know he's here.

'We'll find you some clothes for now,' says Mrs Gideon. 'We'll have to replace the ones you've lost in the fire. It'll be nice to have some new things, won't it?'

Then it sinks in. There is nothing left. The flat is burnt out. There's no table or chairs, or beds, or clothes. No *Titanic* DVD.

Those things don't matter, but there are other things that can't be replaced.

The feathers. Red's feathers.

All his feathers will have burnt; been charred and turned to dust. All the beautiful colours are gone. Red won't have his feathers to connect him to our world. He won't have his feathers to help him fly.

'Red needs me,' I say.

'Have this.' Mrs Gideon passes me the mug of hot chocolate.

Renée folds a towel on the bed. 'If you want a shower, the bathroom's down the hall on the left.'

Mrs Gideon nods her head. 'It might feel good to freshen up.'

'Red needs me.' I say it louder this time. I think of him alone, without anyone who knows him, without anyone who understands him.

'Scarlet, we've been through this before. It's complicated. We can't . . . '

I don't let her finish. 'SHUT UP!' I yell. 'JUST SHUT UP!' I hurl the mug against the wall. It shatters in an explosion of splintered china. Hot chocolate sprays across the room, across the duvet and the carpet. I want Renée and the Penguin to shut up and leave me alone. I want their voices out of my head.

'Scarlet . . . '

'SHUT UP!' I cover my head with my arms. 'GO AWAY, GO AWAY, GO AWAY!'

'Scarlet, listen . . . '

I scream to block them out.

'GO AWAY . . . GO AWAY . . . GO AWAY!'

I scream to block all my thoughts.

I scream to block out Red.

I scream so I don't have to think of anything at all.

I scream

and scream,

and scream,

and scream.

CHAPTER 8

I wake to the smell of coffee and the sound of voices drifting up the stairs. The morning sun shines in through the window. I lie in bed and look around me at the hot chocolate stains on the lilac walls, at the tasseled purple lightshade, and the swirls of purple on the curtains. A sweatshirt and a twin pack of leggings are folded on the chair next to me. There's a wash bag with toothbrush and toothpaste too. The clothes still have the supermarket labels attached. Renée must have bought them for me last night.

I swing my legs out of bed and try to wipe the sleep from my eyes. My whole body aches with tiredness, and I'm starving. I haven't eaten anything since yesterday lunchtime. Little Red won't have eaten anything either. I look across to the corner of the room, but my schoolbag has gone. I can't see it anywhere in the room at all.

I get dressed and go down the stairs. I stand in the doorway of the kitchen. Another family's kitchen. I'm a stranger here.

Renée's husband is sitting at the table, drinking coffee, and tapping on a laptop. Jez, the boy in the photo, is slumped across a bowl of cereal. He's wearing a T-shirt and boxer shorts and looks like he's just crawled out of bed. Renée's putting toast onto the table. She turns and smiles. 'Morning, Scarlet. Sleep well?'

I look around the room. 'Where's the chick?'

Renée glances at her husband, and then at me. 'You mean the one in your bag?'

I scowl at them. What a stupid question. What other one do they think I mean?

'It was making a terrible mess in there,' says Renée. 'Theo's taken it out to the garage for now.'

'He needs food,' I say. 'He lost his mother in the fire.'

Renée pulls out a chair. 'Why don't you sit down and have some breakfast first. We can take the chick to the vet's later. They might take it in.'

'No. He can't go there. *I* have to look after him.'

Silence fills the kitchen. All three of them are staring at me.

'He's mine,' I say. 'He needs food.'

'Well . . . ' Renée begins. She glances at Theo, as if she's working out the right thing to say, but it's Jez who gets up from the table.

He grabs a piece of toast and pushes back his chair. 'Come on then,' he says. 'Let's feed your chick.'

Renée's eyes open wide, but she doesn't say anything. She just watches as I follow Jez outside.

It's cold in the garage. We find the chick in a cardboard box. It's sitting on old newspapers, hunched against one side in a pool of his own mess. His eyes are closed and he's only taking shallow breaths. I kneel down and scoop him onto my hand. He feels clammy and weak, and his head flops forward on his chest.

'He's too cold,' I say. 'He needs to come inside.'

Jez makes a snorting sound. 'Mum hates birds. She's got a thing about them. It's all the flapping and the feathers.'

I frown. Red would hate it here. I stroke the soft feathers on the chick's chest. 'He'll die out here.'

Jez sighs. 'Try this.' He crumbles a piece of toast for me to feed. 'So, how come you've rescued a pigeon?'

'Found him,' I say. I push some crumbs into his beak. At first Little Red isn't interested, but he swallows them back and looks for more.

Scarlet Ibis

Jez passes me more crumbs. 'Seems you're pretty keen on him. What's his name?'

I glance across at Jez. He seems OK, but I don't know if I can trust him. I shrug my shoulders. 'He doesn't have one.' I don't want to tell anyone his name, because only Red and I know. It's our secret, and I want there to be some things no one can take from us.

Renée finds us covering Little Red's box with an old coat to keep him warm.

'Come on, Jez,' she calls, 'you're not even dressed. Don't be late for the bus.'

Inside the house, Jez disappears upstairs and I follow Renée into the kitchen.

'Come and have some breakfast,' says Renée.

I pull out a chair and sit down. I take a sideways look at Theo. He looks like Jez, but older, and a bit fatter. A badge on his green uniform says *Senior Nursing Officer*.

Renée pours me a glass of orange juice and offers me some toast. I'm spreading jam when Jez appears again. His school blazer's crumpled and his tie hangs loose around his neck.

Renée puts her hand on her hips. 'You can't go to school like that, look at yourself.'

'Keep cool, Mum. It's no big deal.'

'You've got to get up earlier.'

Jez drinks my glass of orange juice and grabs another piece of toast. 'Scientific fact. The teenage brain needs more sleep.'

'Well then,' says Renée, pouring me another glass of juice. 'You can get to bed earlier. You can't play gigs late into the night with your exams coming up.'

Jez shoves the toast in his mouth and frowns at her.

She waggles her finger at him. 'If you're not careful, you're going to waste that mind of yours.'

Jez shakes his head and looks across at me. 'Things must be bad where you live to end up here. I didn't think it could get worse than this.'

'Jez!' his mum snaps. She glares at him, a long hard glare. 'It's time you went to school.'

Jez leans down for his school bag. 'Nice to meet you, Scarlet,' he says. He nods in the direction of his mum and winks at me. 'And good luck!'

Renée watches him leave the room. We hear the front door slam and she breathes out. She's shaking her head but smiling. 'So, now you've met my son, Jez. *The* laziest boy in the *whole* wide world.'

*

Scarlet Ibis

Mrs Gideon turns up mid-morning. She's in penguin mode again. I don't ask her about going to school and she doesn't mention it. I guess there are more important things she wants to talk about today. I follow her and Renée into the kitchen and slump against the wall, warming my legs on the radiator.

Mrs Gideon sits and folds her arms. She looks at me over the top of her glasses. 'The good news is that I can take you to see your mother today.'

My head snaps up. 'Today? Now?' I can't believe it.

Mrs Gideon smiles. 'Yes, I've had it cleared with the review panel.'

'And Red?' I say. 'Am I seeing him too?'

She pauses for a moment before she speaks. 'Not yet, Scarlet. It's more complicated with Red.'

'He needs me until Mum gets out of hospital, until we can live back together again.'

'Scarlet,' she says. 'Sit down.'

I pull a chair out and sit opposite her. Renée sits down too and wraps her hands around her mug of tea.

'Scarlet,' says Mrs Gideon again. The Penguin's voice is low and heavy. 'Your mum is not well enough at the moment to look after either you or Red.'

'We'll be fine,' I say. 'I can look after us all until she's better.'

'Scarlet, you're only twelve. You're just a child. Red relies far too much on you. He doesn't communicate with anyone but you. It's not fair for you, or him.'

I hate the way Penguins think they know best. 'I've managed so far,' I say. I hear my voice rising. 'I can cook and clean and change beds as good as any adult. I can take Red to school and help him with his homework. I *can* do it. I know I can.'

Mrs Gideon leans forward. 'It's not your responsibility. Your mother is not well enough to look after you. You deserve a childhood. You deserve to muck about and play with friends. You need help with your schoolwork, too.'

I lean forward so that my face is close to hers. 'I'm fine. You've seen my school reports. I can look after us all, I've been doing it for years.'

She sighs and folds her hands together. 'Scarlet, you are not safe at home.'

I stand up and push the chair back. 'It wasn't Mum's fault our flat caught fire.'

Mrs Gideon's silent for a moment, as if deciding what to say. 'Scarlet, your mother fell asleep in bed with a cigarette in her hand. The sheets caught fire.'

My hands feel cold and clammy. My heart is pumping in my chest, but my head is light and the room spins around me. I'm back in the flat, the morning I left them. I hear Mum asking me for a cup of tea in bed and her lighter.

Her lighter.

I fall back down into my chair. 'It wasn't Mum's fault,' I say. I now know the truth and it makes me feel sick deep down inside. 'It was mine.'

Mrs Gideon frowns. 'You weren't even there.'

'Exactly,' I say. 'I should have been there. I should have stayed home to look after Red. If I hadn't given Mum the lighter, it wouldn't have been in her bedroom.' I look from the Penguin to Renée, but they still don't seem to understand. 'Don't you get it?' I shout. I slam my hands on the table. 'This is all *my* fault.'

I sit in Mrs Gideon's car as she drives me to the hospital. She tries to tell me that I'm not to blame, that Mum is too ill to look after us. But I keep going over that day. If only I'd stayed at home, none of this would have happened. It was only a stupid theatre company. I could have seen it another time. Now we've got nowhere to live, Mum's in hospital, and I don't know where Red is at all.

Stupid, stupid me.

'We're here,' says Mrs Gideon. 'We can't be too long.'

I follow Mrs Gideon into lifts and along corridors, until we reach a ward with eight beds, four along each side. I see Mum in the bed by the window. She's propped up on pillows and she's looking out across the rooftops.

Mrs Gideon draws a curtain to screen us from the other beds and I sit next to Mum.

'Mum?' I say.

Mum turns. She frowns for a moment, as if she doesn't recognize my face, and then she smiles. 'Scarlet!'

I put out my hand and she holds it in hers.

'I'm sorry,' I say.

Mum rubs my hands. Her hair is lank and greasy. It could do with a wash. I want to take her home and look after her. I hate seeing her like this.

'Are you OK?' I say.

'I'm fine,' she says. She coughs, a deep retching cough, and I don't know if it's from the cigarettes or the fire smoke. Her words are blurred and mumbled, and I wonder if she's on extra medication. She reaches for something beneath her pillow. 'I've been waiting for you to come,' she says. 'I saved something.' She smiles a secret smile.

Maybe she's saved Red's scarlet ibis feather. I lean forward to see, but it's not the feather that Mum saved. It's the faded photo she always clings to. The photo of my dad.

Scarlet Ibis

She runs her finger across his face. 'Couldn't lose him, could we?'

I stare at the man in the photo. He means nothing to me. I don't know him at all. If anything, I hate him. I hate him for leaving us. I hate him for leaving Mum. I wouldn't want to find him even if I could.

'How's Red?' I ask.

Mum looks up and frowns. 'Red?'

'Have you seen him?'

She looks across at Mrs Gideon. 'How *is* Red?'

I see Mrs Gideon shift from one foot to the other. 'Red is out of hospital, and he's being cared for.'

I just stare at Mum. She hadn't asked about Red at all. She didn't try to save him. Maybe she didn't even think about him. All she wanted from the flat was that stupid photograph.

I stand up. 'I'm ready to go,' I say.

'So soon?' asks Mum.

'I have to get back.'

Mrs Gideon shoulders her bag and looks between us, but my thoughts are jumbled in my head and I can't sort them out at all.

'Scarlet?'

But I don't want to listen.

I don't want to stay here a moment longer than I have to. I turn from Mum and Mrs Gideon, and walk away.

Chapter 9

'Do you like stir-fries?' Renée holds up a bag of beansprouts.

'I think so,' I say

'Good.' She smiles. 'Jez will be back from school soon and stir-fries are always quick to do.'

I help her in the kitchen, slicing the chicken, grating ginger, and laying the table for the four of us: Renée, Theo, Jez, and me. I'm relieved she doesn't ask any questions about my visit to see Mum. I don't want to talk about it today. My mind can't work it all out. I let her do the talking. She tells me about her job as a part-time schoolteacher, and about Jez and Avril, and how Avril's doing at uni, and how she misses her. She talks so proudly of them, even Jez.

'Speak of the devil,' Renée says.

We hear a rap at the door, and Jez's voice yelling through the letterbox to be let in.

'Hi Mum. Hi Scarlet.' Jez dumps his bags on the floor and turns to me. 'How's the chick?'

'He's OK,' I say. 'I gave him some more bread, but he's not eaten much of it.'

'Birdseed,' he says, reaching for the biscuit tin. 'That's what he needs. You'll get some, won't you, Mum?'

His mum slaps him on the hand. 'No biscuits now. Go and get changed and call your dad. Scarlet's made supper today and it'll be ready in five minutes.'

Renée turns to me once Jez has left the room, 'Scarlet . . . about the pigeon . . . '

'What?'

She puts her hand on my shoulder, but I shrug it off. 'We just can't keep it here.'

'Why not?'

'Because . . . well, they carry diseases for a start . . . and it'll make a mess . . . ' her voice trails off as Jez and Theo come in to the kitchen.

I know she won't let me keep Little Red. She doesn't even like birds. But if Little Red doesn't start eating, he won't last much longer anyway. I can't let Red's pigeon die. It's the only thing that connects me with him.

Scarlet Ibis

I just eat and listen to the talk around the table. I let their words flow over me. I'm an outsider, listening in. I hear Jez arguing with his mum, and Theo laughing at them both. I hear the clatter of knives and forks against plates, and the glug of water poured from the jug.

When Theo has finished, he sits back and squeezes his wife's hand. 'That was the best meal you've made for ages, love.' He gives me a sly smile. 'Your cooking's improving. Now, if you'll excuse me, I've got some work to catch up on.'

I help Renée to clear away the plates and put them in the dishwasher. I wipe the placemats and put them away in a drawer. All this time, I notice Jez is just sitting, watching me.

When the phone rings, Renée answers it and walks into the hall to speak.

It's just Jez and me in the kitchen. I feel his eyes on me as I rinse the saucepans in the sink and put them in the dishwasher. I start to wipe the surfaces with a cloth, but Jez gets up and goes to the door between the kitchen and the hall. He closes it and presses his back against it.

I stop what I'm doing and look at him.

'You can't stay,' he says.

I feel my mouth go dry.

He shakes his head. 'I don't want you here.'

I twist the dishcloth in my hand. I don't know what to say. I thought he liked me, but maybe he was just putting it on in front of his mum and dad. Maybe he's been waiting for this moment, when we're alone.

He takes a step towards me. 'It's not going to work, you being here. You know that, don't you?'

For every step he takes forward, I step back, until I feel my spine against the work surface.

Jez leans down and starts taking plates and cutlery from the dishwasher, scattering them on the work surfaces.

'They've not been washed,' I say.

Jez nods sagely. 'I know. That's the point. You see . . . ' he says.

I see the corners of his mouth start to twitch, like he's trying not to laugh.

He leans forward and points at his chest. 'You are showing me up *big* time.' He's laughing now, deep belly laughs. 'If you carry on like this, Mum will make *me* do all the housework too. You'll ruin years and years of hard work perfecting the art of laziness.'

I just glare at him, but it makes him laugh even more.

He's holding his sides. 'The look on your face!'

His head's thrown back and his mouth's wide open, laughing at me. I'm so mad at him, I chuck the dirty dishcloth and it hits him smack in the face. He stops laughing and looks so shocked that's it's my turn to laugh.

Jez wipes the bits of rice from his face. A yellow stain dribbles down his white shirt.

He shakes his head and fills a glass of water to the brim. 'Right Scarlet,' he grins. 'You know what this means . . . ' He swings his arm, letting the water fly in a wide arc towards me. 'This means war.'

CHAPTER 10

I couldn't let Jez get away with getting me wet, so I had to soak him, too. By the time Renée finishes her phone call, there's water everywhere and a cracked plate on the floor.

She just stands in the doorway, arms folded across her chest, glaring at Jez. 'Having fun?'

Jez pulls a face of innocence and points at me. 'She started it!'

I spin round at him. 'Did not!'

Jez starts packing plates into the dishwasher. 'I was just clearing away, trying to help, when she started chucking water at me.'

The corner of Renée's mouth curls up in a smile. 'Really, Jez? Of course you were! Well, in that case, don't let me stop you. You can finish here, while I chat to Scarlet about a few things.'

I skirt around Jez and follow Renée into the sitting room, taking a seat on the sofa.

Renée pulls up a footstool and sits in front of me, her hands pressed between her knees. 'Scarlet, that was Jo on the phone.'

'Mrs Gideon, you mean?'

Renée nods.

I frown at her. 'And?'

'How would you feel about staying here with us a little longer?'

'How much longer?'

She shrugs her shoulders. 'Until your mother is well enough to look after you.'

I fold my hands together and stare at them. 'What if she's never well enough?'

Renée sighs. She doesn't answer. Maybe she doesn't know the answer. Maybe no one does.

She takes my hands in hers. 'The review panel have just had a meeting about you and they think that it might be best for you to have a long-term foster placement.'

'Here?' I say.

Renée nods. 'Would that be OK with you?'

I just stare at her hands wrapped around mine.

She leans forward. 'You would still be able to see your mother and stay in contact with her.'

I close my eyes and try to squeeze back the tears, but they slide in large drops down my cheeks and fall into my lap.

I'm losing everything, Mum and Red and home. I'm losing everything I ever knew. It's all spinning away from me, spinning into other orbits, and I can't make it stop.

Renée slides next to me on the sofa and wraps her arm around me. 'Scarlet, you are welcome here. I know it's not what you want, but at the moment you need somewhere to stay so you can be safe and go to school.'

'School?'

'Jo thinks it is too far to travel to your old school. She suggested that you could go to Jez's school. Maybe it would be a new start.'

A new start. A new family. A new life. Do I pretend I don't have a family of my own?

Renée reaches into a wicker basket of magazines. She rummages in the bottom and pulls out a brochure. 'You can have Avril's room,' she says. 'Maybe you'd like to have a look at some paints and decide what colour you'd like in your room. It needs a freshen up.'

Scarlet Ibis

I think of the hot chocolate stains on the wall and carpet, and feel bad about them. I start flicking through the paint charts, reading all the different paint names and their suggested colour combinations: forest fern, lavender haze, burnt caramel, dairy cream.

'Is that why Red and I can't be together. We have to be colour matched? I'm with you and he's with some white family?'

Renée shakes her head. 'It doesn't work like that any more.'

'So why isn't he here? Why can't we be together? No one will even tell me where he is.'

'Scarlet, it isn't up to me.'

I chuck the brochure back in the basket. 'It should be up to Red and *me*. But no one listens to us, do they? They do what they think's best.'

Renée sighs. 'It's complicated. Red is being assessed. At the moment he's a danger to himself. He puts himself at risk.'

I glare at her. 'What d'you mean?'

She takes her time to answer, as if she's not sure what to say or how to say it. 'The day of the fire, a neighbour of yours went in to save your mum and Red.'

'Mrs Kanwar, yes, I know.'

'Well,' says Renée, 'she says Red wouldn't leave his bedroom. He was trying to climb out of the window. He kept shouting *Red must fly. Red must fly.*'

I just stare at her. I think back to the time he stood on the window ledge with the wings Sita and I made for him. But *I* knew he wouldn't jump. He was just feeling the wind beneath his wings.

'Scarlet,' says Renée. Her voice is soft and sympathetic. 'Red is a complex child. He has different needs.'

'Tell me about it!' I push her away and get up from the sofa. 'You're right. He does have different needs.' I ram my finger against my chest. 'He needs me.'

CHAPTER 11

I stand in the hallway and wait for Jez. I look at myself in the mirror. Grey blazer. Grey skirt. Black tights. I'm glad Renée found me some second-hand uniform. I don't want to look shiny new and conspicuous on my first day at school. I don't even want to go. I want to stay and look after Little Red. He's quieter than usual, and just sits in the corner of his box.

'OK,' says Jez, 'let's go.'

I follow Jez along the road to the bus stop. I turn to see Renée standing in the doorway, twisting a tea towel round and round her hands. She lifts one hand in a final wave before she closes the door. Mrs Gideon has given me leaflets on how to deal with racism and bullying. She says some 'looked after' kids can have a rough time. I guess that's me. I've got that label now.

I stand with Jez and watch the school bus loom into view and crawl towards us in the morning traffic. I feel sick with dread. New people. New school. And questions, questions, questions.

We're one of the last pick-ups on the route, and the school bus is full. I feel everyone's eyes watching me as I follow Jez to the back of the bus where his friends sit. I guess Jez must be considered 'cool' to sit back here.

His friends budge up for us.

'Hi guys,' he says, flopping down. 'Meet Scarlet.'

I'm not sure what to do or say, so I give a small smile.

'Scarlet,' says Jez, 'meet my band members, Fish and Reggie.'

Fish is tall and lanky, with greasy skin and spiky blonde hair. Reggie has wave patterns shaved close to his head, and is one of the few other black kids on the bus.

'Hi, Scarlet,' says Fish. 'How come you're stuck with Jez?'

Jez puts his arm around my shoulder. 'Scarlet's staying with us, while her mum's in hospital.'

I stare down at the floor. So this is it. This is when they find out I'm in care. This is when they find out about Mum too. I glance across at Jez. I'll be the girl with the nut-case mother in a loony bin.

Scarlet Ibis

Jez turns and winks so only I can see. 'She's my little baby cousin.'

Fish and Reggie look at each other. Fish narrows his eyes. 'You don't look related,' he says. He leans closer for a better look. 'I guess Jez got the ugly gene.'

Jez gives him a shove, and then they start talking about their band and music and school stuff. I look out of the window and watch the streets pass in a blur.

Jez just did me one huge favour. I'm not in care.

I'm his cousin.

I'm family.

I belong.

And somehow, that gives me my protection.

CHAPTER 12

I walk along the corridor to the first lesson after being introduced to my tutor group at registration. Two girls I recognize from the bus walk with me.

'So, you're Jez's cousin?'

I nod.

One girl pushes loose hair from her face. 'Cool.' She says. 'Are you in Tin Road?'

'Tin Road?' I say.

'*Tin Road*, his band?'

I shake my head. Maybe I don't know enough about Jez to keep this lie going.

'I'm Erin, by the way,' she says. 'And this is Gracie.'

I nod and smile. I'm being jostled along the corridor, pressed in by all the other kids.

Scarlet Ibis

'How long are you staying with Jez?' says Gracie.

'Till mum's better,' I say.

'What's the matter with her?'

I feel hot and crushed in. Erin and Gracie are either side of me, waiting for an answer. 'Cancer,' I say. 'Mum's got cancer.'

Gracie's eyes open wide. 'That sucks. My auntie died of that.'

Erin grabs my arm as we walk into class. 'Come on Scarlet, sit with us at the back. You don't want to be anywhere near Mrs Atkins. She's dead boring and even worse, she stinks. You can smell her from three desks back.'

I sit between Erin and Gracie and stare out of the window. A flock of pigeons wheels across the houses, their storm-coloured feathers dark against the pale sky. I've told another lie. It's easier this way. Sometimes I wish Mum had cancer instead. When Amy Johns's mum had cancer, everyone said how brave she was, how she fought it like a soldier going into battle. Everyone joined her army. The flags were flying, the bugles called. She marched into battle with an army of followers fighting right there alongside her, lifting her up high.

But with Mum's illness, there are no flags or bugle calls.

There are no back-up troops.

No medals given out for bravery.

It's just us.

Alone.

And it's lonely on our battlefield.

Erin and Gracie want to take me under their wing. I'm Jez's cousin, so I'm cool. My mum's got cancer, so that makes me kind of special. I'm a novelty. Tragic. Interesting. For now, at least. I'm writing out a new script for my life and rubbing out the past. A new life. A lie. A new me. Is this what happens when you step into someone else's life and leave behind your own? What if I'm asked about my family? Do I write Red out of my new life too?

We have maths, then English, and then break. I've already got two pieces of homework to do so I slip back to the tutor room. I'm just opening my maths book when Erin finds me.

'Scarlet, what are you *doing*?'

'Thought I'd get homework out of the way.'

Erin rolls her eyes and stuffs my maths book into my bag. 'Don't be such a geek. Come on, Tamsin wants to meet you.' She leans into me, and whispers, 'come and meet the Rooftop Gang.'

I follow Erin across the playground, to the bike sheds in the far corner of the school grounds. They back onto the concrete P.E. block. Some of the bike racks are missing, and I see Gracie and three other girls sitting up on top of the bike-shed roof.

A tall girl with white-blonde hair lets a ladder down.

I follow Erin up on to the roof, and the girl pulls the ladder up behind us.

'Hi guys,' says Erin. 'This is Scarlet.'

They all look at me. Gracie's there already, so I guess she's told them all about me. The white-blonde girl is the first one to speak. 'Hi Scarlet,' she says. 'I'm Tamsin, Fish's sister. You've met Gracie, and this is Laura and Kim.'

Tamsin looks like her brother, with her blonde hair, pale blue eyes, and pale skin—but without the spots. I sit down at the edge of their circle.

Tamsin passes round a pack of biscuits. 'They're only three weeks out of date,' she says. 'Better than last time.'

Erin takes a biscuit and passes the packet on to me. 'Tamsin's dad owns a newsagents. He's always giving us his out of date stuff.'

I listen to them talk about school and other kids and teachers. I work out the teachers who let you hand in homework late, which ones are nice, and which ones to avoid. Tamsin shows us the new shoes she's bought for school.

'Now *those* are killer heels,' says Laura.

'You'll never get those past Miss P,' says Gracie.

'I'll walk behind you all,' Tamsin laughs. 'She won't even see.'

They talk about clothes and what they want to buy, and I hope Renée will let me get some new clothes too. I'm glad I'm wearing uniform. At least it doesn't show me up.

A pigeon flutters down and struts near us, its head tilted, watching us for dropped crumbs. I crumble the edges of my biscuit and drop the pieces near my feet. The pigeon paces closer, not trusting enough to come too close. If Red were here, it would trust him. He's so quiet and still with birds, he almost becomes invisible. I sometimes wish I could be invisible too.

'Hey Scarlet! You'll have to watch out for Baba Yaga.'

I frown, 'Baba Yaga?'

Tamsin nods. 'Baba Yaga, the old Russian witch. She likes pigeons too. She comes to feed them in the park.'

Gracie grabs my arm and pulls me down. 'Look,' she hisses. 'That's her now.'

We all flatten ourselves on the roof and watch the old woman walking along the pavement on the far side of the road. She doesn't look like a witch. She's carrying plastic bags which swing back and forth as she lurches along. Her

Scarlet Ibis

face is hidden behind a headscarf, and she's wrapped in a shawl and an old coat. Long woollen socks are wrinkled around her thick ankles, and her feet are stuffed into cut-off rubber boots.

Tamsin narrows her eyes. 'She's evil. She turns children into birds.'

'Tamsin!' laughs Kim. 'We used to tell that story in primary school.'

Tamsin's eyes open wide. 'It's no joke. Naseem disappeared last year. What happened to him?'

Laura rolls her eyes. 'His family moved to Birmingham.'

Tamsin leans in closer to the circle. 'So we were told. But children go missing all the time. Baba Yaga turns them into birds. She boils them down and eats them with her iron teeth.'

We watch the woman hobble along the street and stop at the end house. She puts her bags down and fumbles for her keys before letting herself in and closing the door behind her.

Erin breathes out and sits back up. 'That's her house. It's full of birds. When you walk past you can hear them flapping against the windows.'

Tamsin nods. Her eyes are wide, wide open. She's enjoying this story. 'It's true. You can hear them scratching and pecking. They're all children, trapped in there, trying to get out.'

Gracie snorts a laugh. 'I told my little brother I'd take him to Baba Yaga if he ever messed up my room again. You should have seen his face.'

I can't help smiling and notice Tamsin sees me.

She frowns. 'Don't laugh. It's true.' She keeps her voice to a whisper, so everyone has to lean in closer. 'Rumour has it, that if she offers you a chocolate you're done for. She's chosen you. She's going turn you into one of her bird children and keep you there for ever.'

The end of break bell wakes us from Tamsin's story. I grab my bag to go.

'Hey, Scarlet,' says Tamsin.

We all turn to look at her. 'D'you want to be in the Rooftop Gang?'

I look around the faces. This is my first chance of making friends and I don't want to blow it.

I nod.

Tamsin gives a sly smile. 'Then you have to do a dare.'

Gracie frowns. 'We could let her off. Her mum's ill, after all.'

Scarlet Ibis

Tamsin shakes her head. 'Rules is rules, Gracie. You know that.'

I look around them. 'What kind of dare?'

'I reckon,' says Tamsin, a sly smile creeping across her face. 'I reckon Scarlet should get into Baba Yaga's house and bring something back to prove it.'

'No way,' says Gracie.

'Come on, Tamsin,' says Laura. 'Not even you would do that.'

Erin's looking between me and Tamsin, seeing who will win.

Tamsin shoulders her bag. 'That's the dare,' she says She turns to me, challenge in her eyes. 'You don't think she's a witch, so it should be a problem. I'm sure she's just a harmless little old lady.'

'It's too risky,' says Gracie. 'Let's dare her to take something from the staffroom instead.'

Tamsin puts her hands on her hips. 'What is it with you lot? Lost your bottle?'

She glares at them. Kim picks at some moss growing in the cracks in the roof. Gracie stares down at her hands.

Erin is just watching, waiting.

I don't want them to think I'm chicken. 'I'll do it,' I say. They all look at me.

'I'll do it. I'll go.'

Tamsin looks triumphant. She grins. 'Good on you, Scarlet. Tomorrow lunchtime. Let's all meet here, and we'll watch you go to Baba Yaga's house.'

I smile deep inside. I don't want to be alone any more. I want friends. I want to be in their gang too.

CHAPTER 13

It's not until Friday lunchtime that I get to do the dare. The teachers have been prowling in the playground all week, standing near the gates. I haven't had a chance, until now.

Tamsin stands up tall on the bike-shed roof. 'OK,' she says. 'It's only Mrs Bentley on duty today. Laura's going to distract her by pretending to be sick, so you can get out of the gates. We'll watch you from up here.'

'What if Baba Yaga's not in,' I say.

'She'll be in,' says Tamsin. 'She goes to feed the birds first thing in the morning. She'll be back by now.'

'OK,' I say. 'I'm ready.' I slide my hands deep in my pockets. I do my best to look almost bored, like it's no big deal, but my palms are slick with sweat.

Gracie glances between Tamsin and me. 'I don't think this is such a great idea. I mean, what if . . . ' her voice trails off.

Tamsin leans forward and grins. 'What if Baba Yaga offers Scarlet a chocolate? What then?' She makes squawking sounds and flaps her hands, just like a bird.

Erin, Laura, and Kim screech with laughter. Gracie smiles but glances at me, biting the corner of her lip.

Tamsin gives Laura a shove and points to Mrs Bentley. 'OK Laura, you know what to do.'

We watch Laura climb down the ladder and walk across the playground towards Mrs Bentley. Laura clutches her stomach and doubles over. It's the worst acting I've seen, but Mrs Bentley seems convinced. She glances around the playground, checking it all looks quiet and under control, and steers Laura inside the school.

This is my chance. I walk along the wire fencing, hands in pockets. Casual. When I reach the gates, I don't even look around to see if anyone has seen me. I slip out and cross the road, walking with my head down, on the far side of the street, on my way to Baba Yaga's house.

I can feel Tamsin, Erin, Gracie and Kim watching me from the bike shed roof. If I look at them I might chicken out, so I focus on the house at the end of the street.

Scarlet Ibis

I stop outside the plain white door. There's a window to the right, and two windows upstairs with their curtains drawn. Net curtains screen the downstairs room. I could pretend to knock, and walk away and make them think Baba Yaga isn't in. Maybe that's what I'll do. But I won't have done the dare. I'll have to do it again and I might not be brave enough next time.

I can't see a bell, so I lift my hand and knock three times.

Knock.

Knock.

Knock.

THUD!

Something hits the inside of the window to my right, making me jump back. A large seagull lifts the edge of the net curtain and struts up and down the windowsill, watching me. It cocks its head from side to side. I can't help staring at its yellow eyes. Its feathers are greenish white and look brittle and frayed, not like the snow-soft feathers of the seagulls on the river. It throws its head back and gives a mewling cry. Erin was right. She said she'd seen birds flapping at the windows.

Other than the seagull, there's no sign of life. Maybe

Baba Yaga is out after all. I turn the handle of the door, expecting it to be locked, but it keeps turning and I push the door open just a crack.

I peer in.

Boxes of old newspapers line the hallway. Plastic containers filled with seeds are neatly stacked against the walls. The house smells like a mixture of boiled cabbage, disinfectant, and the aviary at the zoo. Baba Yaga's coat is hung over the bannisters at the bottom of the stairs. I can hear the seagull's webbed feet slapping on the floor behind the closed door to my right.

I could just grab one of the old newspapers and go. It wouldn't really be stealing if its yesterday's news. But I can't go. Something draws me in. I slip into the house and shut the door behind me. Ahead of me, at the end of the hall, the door is open. I walk along the tiled floor and peer into a small kitchen. Feed bowls have been washed and stacked on the draining board. Bottles of disinfectant line the windowsill, alongside a pot of miniature daffodils. The kitchen window looks out on to a small patio, crowded with a wooden bench and bird feeders. On the small table in the kitchen, containers full of different foods have name labels: *Petre, Anna-Maria, Lukas, Magda, Sergey, Elena, Marius, Erik, Victor, Michaela* . . .

Scarlet Ibis

So many names.

Everything is spotless.

Everything is quiet.

Everything, except for a pan on the hob. Its lid rattles and steam escapes into the air. This is where Baba Yaga boils her bird-children before she eats them.

It's stupid, I know. Fear makes you believe all sorts of things. It could be anything in the pan. Anything at all. Liquid bubbles over and spits on the metal hob. I look around. Baba Yaga must be in the house somewhere. Maybe she's watching me.

I want to know what's in the pan. I have to know. I move closer and lift the lid. I hold my breath. Steam flies upwards, and when it clears I look in. I breathe out slowly. No bird-children, only three peeled potatoes bouncing around in boiling water.

I leave the lid off and walk back along the hall. I can still hear the seagull pacing on the other side of the door. There are other bird sounds in there too. The harsh caw of a crow. The coo of a dove.

I open the door and push my head through to see. The seagull runs away from me, lifting its wings up high. In the far corner of the room a small TV sits on the floor. The sound is muted. Silent images move across the screen. Along the wall, large plastic boxes with wire grille doors are stacked one on top of the other. They look like the carriers people use to take their cats to the vet, only there must be about fifteen of them. I step closer. Each one contains a bird. I see them inside, moving around, their feathers pressed against the wire door. Some poke their beaks through, looking for food. There are all sorts of birds: pigeons, seagulls, a blackbird, a crow, and lots of smaller finch-type birds. At the end, in a huge cage, is a large black bird smelling of fish. I guess he must be one of the cormorants from the Thames.

I jump when the seagull flaps across to me and pulls at the laces on my shoe.

'Don't mind Petre, he's just saying hello.'

I spin round. I didn't see Baba Yaga right behind me in the armchair. She's sitting perfectly still, wrapped in old blankets so she almost looks like part of the furniture. Her face is deeply lined and she looks old. So old. Wisps of white hair sit on her head like feather-down. Her eyes are small and dark.

'Come on Petre,' she clucks. She lumbers up out of her chair. I check my escape route. She looks old and slow but maybe she's actually fast.

'Remember your manners,' she says. 'It's not often that we have visitors.'

Scarlet Ibis

She must wonder how I got in here. 'The door wasn't locked,' I say.

'No matter,' she says. 'No matter.' She follows Petre to the window where he flaps up on the other side of the net curtain. 'Come on Petre. You've had your run around today, let's put you back.'

Baba Yaga pulls back the corner of the curtain with a bony finger and looks outside. She pauses, looking at the school. 'Those your friends?'

'Yes,' I say. I fiddle with my tie. I know she's looking at Tamsin, Gracie, Erin, and Kim. I know they'll be looking in this direction. I've been ages. They must be wondering what's happened to me.

Baba Yaga drops the curtain and looks at me, her head on her side, just like a bird. 'Didn't they want to come in, too?'

I stare at the floor and say nothing.

'Maybe they sent just you?'

I wonder if she knows this is a dare.

She chuckles, 'And what name do your friends have for me?'

I frown and look at her. 'They say you are called Baba Yaga.'

She shakes her head and stifles a laugh. 'Baba Yaga! Me?'

I take a step away from her. 'Isn't that your name?'

She shuffles closer to me. I can see the bristles on her chin and the pale cloudy blueness of her eyes.

She prods me in the chest. 'Do they mean Baba Yaga . . . the witch from the old Russian fairy tales?'

'I . . . I . . . don't know,' I stammer. I've never heard any Russian fairy tales before.

She grins at me, showing her row of broken teeth and silver fillings. 'Maybe they think I'll boil you down and eat you with my iron teeth?' She turns away, chuckling to herself, repeating the name. 'Baba Yaga . . . Baba Yaga . . .'

I step back towards the door. 'I'd better go.'

Baba Yaga frowns. 'No, please stay. Let your friends worry themselves for a little longer.' She smiles, and her face looks young and mischievous despite the wrinkles. Her small eyes twinkle. 'My name is Madame Popescu. I am Romanian, not Russian.'

'I'm Scarlet,' I say.

Madame Popescu tilts her head to the side. 'It is my pleasure to meet you, Scarlet. I see you've met Petre already.'

The seagull flaps down from the windowsill and runs across the room, his wings held up above him. He flaps up on to the TV, bobbing up and down, opening his beak; daring us to come near him.

Scarlet Ibis

'Petre!' Madame Popescu calls. 'That's enough! She turns to me. 'Petre has always been a spirited one. He came to me when he was only two years old, when he still had his brown mottled feathers. He'd been in an accident and left for dead. I think his stubbornness kept him alive. He can't fly though, poor thing.' She shuffles toward him and chuckles. 'But he makes up for it in voice and spirit!'

I watch her chase Petre into one of the cages, clapping her hands behind him. 'In you go,' she shushes him in and clips the door shut. 'It's Anna-Maria's turn to come out now.'

Madame Popescu reaches into one of the top cages and pulls out a small white dove. It sits cradled in the cup of her hands. 'This is Anna-Maria,' she smiles. 'The sweetest little thing you ever will meet.'

I reach over and stroke the small dove on the head. Her head is crooked sideways as if she can't keep it straight. Her feathers are so soft that I can barely feel them beneath my fingers.

'Here,' says Madame Popescu, putting Anna-Maria in my hands. 'Sit and stroke her for a while.'

I sit down in the armchair and cradle the little dove in my hands. I can feel her gentle cooing against my fingers. I think how Red would love it here.

'She likes you,' says Madame Popescu. 'She's very loving. She was left on my doorstep one morning. She can't walk at all, keeps tilting round in circles. She can't feed herself, so I have to hand-feed her. No one wanted her, it seems. Such a lovely little thing, but the others can pick on her a bit, especially Lukas.' She points to the cormorant in the biggest cage. 'But Lukas had a rough time of it where he came from.'

I stroke Anna-Maria while Madam Popescu talks about all her birds. She tells me about all their different characters. 'They're all my little children,' she beams.

Maybe Tamsin's stories have some truth in them after all. The birds seem as real to her as children. Maybe Red is part bird-child, but got stuck halfway in a spell, neither one nor the other. I wonder what sort of bird she would make of me.

Maybe they really are children.

It's a stupid silly thought. I try to push it away. The tip-tap of the birds' feet in their cages and the squawks and whistles fill the room. I feel trapped, just like the birds. 'I should go,' I say.

'So soon?' says Madame Popescu. 'I wish you didn't have to go. I would love you to stay longer. We don't have many visitors nowadays.' She leans down and pulls a large black box from a bag beside her chair. The box is tied with a pink velvet ribbon. She pulls the ends and opens it. 'It's a special occasion. There's only one left, but I insist you have it.'

I stare into the box. A lone stale chocolate rolls round and round and round.

Madame Popescu pushes the box onto my lap. 'You must have it.' Her eyes are fixed on mine. 'I've never yet met a child who has said no.'

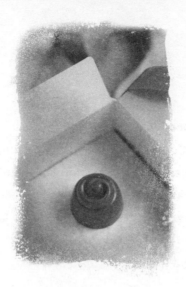

CHAPTER 14

I'm late for afternoon lessons, and it's only when we climb on board the bus back home that I have the chance to tell Tamsin and the others about the dare.

I sit down, squashed between Tamsin and Erin, while Kim, Laura, and Gracie take the seats in front and lean over to look at us.

'What happened?' says Tamsin.

'We almost called the police,' says Kim.

'What was she like?' says Gracie.

'Baba Yaga?' I say. 'Mad bird woman. Completely mad. Mouthful of fillings. Like iron teeth.'

Tamsin sits back and folds her arms. 'Told you, didn't I?'

'Did you see the birds?' asks Erin.

I nod. 'Her house was full of them.'

Scarlet Ibis

Laura's eyes open wide. 'How many birds?'

I stare back at Laura. I'm beginning to enjoy spinning this out, telling them the story they want to hear. 'Loads,' I say. 'Too many to count. They were everywhere, flapping round my head, running round my feet. Bird poo everywhere.'

Gracie pulls a face. 'Ugh! Disgusting!'

Erin shakes her head. 'Shouldn't be allowed.'

'What about the children?' says Tamsin. 'Did you see any children?'

'No children,' I say, 'But . . . ' I look around each of them. Their eyes are fixed on me, waiting to hear what I have to say. I lean closer and lower my voice to a whisper, ' . . . she called each bird by a name . . . a child's name.'

There's a pause as this sinks in.

Laura shudders. 'That's just creepy.'

I look at Tamsin. 'I reckon Tamsin's right,' I say. 'I reckon those birds are children.'

'No way!' says Gracie.

I pull my most serious face. 'She tried it on with me. She tried to make me one of them.'

I see their faces, disbelieving, yet wanting to believe.

'Do you want to know what I took from her house?' I say. I pull the box from my bag. I feel Tamsin and Erin pull away from me, but their eyes are fixed on the box.

I undo the ribbon and open the lid.

Gracie lets out a scream.

I can't help grinning, and pass the box beneath their noses, showing them all. 'I got **The Chocolate,**' I say.

Their eyes are wide, wide open.

'**The Chocolate**!' Gracie repeats.

It rolls round and round the box, clunking against the sides.

'She offered you that?' says Kim.

I nod. 'I didn't eat it. I said I was diabetic, but I'd find another child to give it to. I said I'd find as many children as she wanted.'

'Quick thinking,' says Erin.

Tamsin picks up the chocolate and rolls it between finger and thumb. 'What d'you reckon?' she says. 'Who wants first bite?

'I'm not eating it,' says Kim.

Tamsin pushes it near Erin's mouth. 'I dare you,'

'No way,' says Erin.

Tamsin does the same to all of us. 'Who will dare?' she says, holding the chocolate up high. 'Who will dare try Baba Yaga's chocolate curse?'

A hand reaches down and snatches the chocolate from Tamsin's fingers.

Scarlet Ibis

'If no one wants it, then I'll have to eat it for you,' says Fish.

I look up and watch him pop it in his mouth.

He's grinning at his sister, rolling the chocolate around in his mouth. 'Mmm mmm!' he says. 'De—licious.'

We just stare at him, watching for signs, and his face falls from triumphant to suspicious.

'What?' he says. He stops chewing and looks like he wants to spit it out. 'What's wrong with it?'

'Nothing at all,' Tamsin smiles sweetly. 'Keep eating.'

Fish spits it into his hand. 'Ugh! It's one of Dad's out-of-date stale ones, isn't it?'

Tamsin starts to giggle. 'Yeah! It was going cheap, like you might be.' She flaps her arms and squawks. 'Cheep, cheep, cheep.'

It's such a bad joke, but I can't help laughing.

Fish taps his head with his finger. 'You lot are nuts!'

Our howls of laughter follow him to the back of the bus where he joins Jez and Reggie. He slumps down and scowls at us. I see Jez and Reggie smiling, trying to not laugh at Fish too. I sit back and grin at Tamsin, Erin, Kim, Laura, and Gracie.

I've done it.

I've done the dare.

I'm not alone any more.
I'm one of them now.
I'm in their gang too.

'

CHAPTER 15

'Jez! Scarlet! Get changed.'

We're hardly through the door before Renée is taking our bags and bundling us upstairs. 'Come on you two I said we'd get to Nan's for five.'

Jez pulls a face. 'Nan's?'

Renée nods. 'Had you forgotten? It's her birthday.'

Jez groans. 'I'm meeting Fish and Reggie later. Do I have to go?'

She glares at him. 'Avril's here too. She's come back for the weekend.'

I stop outside my bedroom.

Renée sees me hesitate. 'Don't worry, Scarlet. That's still your room. Avril's staying with Nan.'

*

I walk across the park with Jez and his parents to his nan's house. It's busy in the park. Kids are playing on the climbing frames and swings. People are walking their dogs. The grass is a vivid green and the trees are coming into bud. We could be any other family; mum, dad, brother, and sister.

No one notices us.

We blend in.

Normal.

I feel guilty liking it like this, because it feels like I'm pushing Mum and Red further away. I feel like I've cheated on them. I'm deserting them. I wonder where Red is right now. I imagine him sitting curled up, his arms tight around his head. Perhaps he knows. Perhaps he feels me spreading my wings, getting ready to lift up into the air and fly somewhere where he can't follow.

'You must be Scarlet!'

I'm pulled into a hug by Jez's nan. She's wider than she is tall, and I'm almost suffocated.

'And here's my big boy,' she says, wrapping her arms around Jez. She shakes her head. 'So tall and skinny.' She

Scarlet Ibis

squeezes his arm. 'You need more meat on you.'

I follow them into the house and meet Avril who's stirring pans in the kitchen. The smell of warm spices and coconut fills the air. Avril's tall and slim. Her hair falls in hundreds of braids around her shoulders. Theo puts his arms around his daughter, giving her a huge hug. I can't help staring. I wish I had a dad who'd wrap his arms around me and keep me safe. Avril sees me watching, so I turn away.

'We're eating traditional tonight,' says Nan. Rice and peas, fried plantain, and coconut. I'm cooking my mother's famous tamarind chicken.'

Jez places the presents and cards on the table. 'I can't stay too long, Nan,' he says, looking hard at his mum. 'I'm meeting friends later for a burger.'

Nan shakes her head and tuts. 'I don't know how you eat that rubbish. It's the devil's food.'

Avril gets me to help her with the coconut. I scrape the hard white coconut meat from inside its shell into a bowl.

Nan picks up the shell and turns it over in her hand. 'You'd think we'd be able to get fresh coconut in the supermarkets nowadays, not like this old thing,' she tuts.

'What wrong with it?' I say.

'What's wrong with it?' Nan pulls out a chair and sits down next to me. 'I'll tell you what's wrong with it.'

I smile, because I have the feeling I'm in for a story.

Nan picks at the tough brown fibres on the hard shell. 'When I grew up we had fresh coconut every day. My brother would climb up a tree outside our house and knock them down. They were young green coconuts, not these hard old brown things. Inside was the sweetest coconut milk. But the best bit,' she says, nodding her head, 'was the coconut jelly. Not this hard white stuff, but sweet soft coconut. We'd scrape it from the inside of the shell with our fingers. Mmm! Mmm! I can taste it now.'

Jez reaches across to pinch a piece of coconut.

His nan leans forward. 'Did I tell you about the time my father got hit on the head by a coconut?'

Jez rolls his eyes. 'Yes, Nan. Just a few times.'

'I haven't heard it,' I say.

Nan leans back, folds her hands on her stomach, and smiles. 'Now, there's a story,' she says. 'Maybe I'll save it for after supper.'

While Renée and Nan fuss in the kitchen preparing supper, Avril offers to braid my hair. I sit on the floor in front of her and let her pull her fingers and a wide comb through my hair.

'So, is my little brother behaving himself?' she says.

Scarlet Ibis

I smile. 'Jez is OK.'

'And school? Is that OK? Does Miss P still straighten everyone's tie?'

'She's pretty strict,' I say.

'Doesn't sound like it's changed much since I left,' says Avril.

'I'm sorry I've got your room,' I say. 'You can have it back.'

'No worries,' says Avril. 'I like staying with Nan. She loves the company since Poppa died. Besides, it's a lot quieter without Jez about and I can get some study done. I don't know how you put up with him.'

Jez looks across at her. 'Yeah? Well maybe I prefer Scarlet as a sister! She doesn't nag me or spend hours in the bathroom.'

Avril lobs the comb at him. 'Just let me know if he causes you any trouble, Scarlet, and I'll come and sort him out.'

Jez pulls a face at Avril and flicks on the TV.

I smile and close my eyes. I lean back against Avril while she splits my hair into sections and threads beads onto different strands. I feel her fingers working through my scalp and it almost sends me into sleep.

'Hey, beautiful!' Avril shifts around to look at me. 'Want

to see yourself in the mirror?'

I get up and run my hands down my braids. My hair feels so different, lighter, but heavy at the same time.

Avril's nan comes in and holds me at arm's length, inspecting me. 'Mmm, mmm,' she says. 'You're gonna break some hearts one day.'

'Come on,' smiles Avril. 'Come and have a look.'

I follow her into the bathroom and look in the mirror. I don't recognize myself. I look older. Different. I touch my face, not quite believing what I see. I run my fingers down the braids and along the smooth line of my jaw.

I smile, and feel strangely shy at my own reflection.

I look right into my dark brown eyes.

Maybe this really is me.

Maybe I am beautiful.

I've never thought about myself like that before.

After supper, I sit and listen to Nan recount the stories of her childhood in Jamaica. I hear how her father was knocked out cold by a coconut and couldn't remember anything for two whole weeks. I hear about her coming to London with her parents and growing up in the East End.

I can tell the others have heard these stories a thousand

times before. Avril chats to her mum about life at uni. Jez taps on his phone. Theo reads the paper. They don't have to listen because the stories have become part of them, part of who they are. But *I* listen. Neither Red nor I have stories like these to anchor us. I don't know anything about my dad, and I've never met Mum's parents. They threw her out not long after she had me. Red and I have no past to cling to. There is nothing to tell us who we are or where we came from. It feels like we've been cut adrift and lost in the middle of the sea.

CHAPTER 16

Renée and Avril take me shopping at the weekend.
Renée buys me jeans and tops and new trainers. Renée
gives me twenty pounds too, to buy something special, but
I don't want to spend it just on me. I've never had that
much money for myself before. I'll save it for Red and Mum,
when we're together again. Avril buys me a necklace with
a guardian angel pendant. She fastens it around my neck.
'To watch over you and help you keep Jez under control,'
she smiles.

They fuss over me all weekend, and I know they're trying
to be kind, but the truth is, I want some time to myself.

I'm worried about Little Red, too. At first he ate loads
of breadcrumbs, but he's been taking less and less food
all week. I've tried him on cereal and birdseed. Theo

even brought back a syringe from work for me to try and give him water. But Little Red hasn't grown at all since he's been here. Before, Red and I could see him growing almost every day. Now he just sits lifeless in the cardboard box. By Monday morning, he doesn't try to take any food at all.

Renée puts her head around the garage door. 'Scarlet, time for school.'

I stare into the box. 'He won't eat.'

Renée takes a few steps closer and peers in. She wrinkles her nose. 'You've done your best Scarlet. He's very young.' She puts her hand on my shoulder. 'Sometimes nature just has to take its course.'

'No,' I say. I feel tears burn in my eyes. I don't want Renée to see me cry. I can't give up on Little Red. I'd feel like I was giving up on Red too.

'I'll take him to the vet today,' says Renée. 'They'll know what's best to do.' She gently pulls my arm. 'Come on, Scarlet. Time to go.'

I wait for Jez at the bottom of the stairs and slump on the bottom step. I don't want Renée to take Little Red to the vet's. He's just another pigeon. London's overrun with pigeons. Why would they bother with him?

Little Red needs someone to look after him. Someone

who knows just what he needs. I can't keep him here, but there's one place I know where I could take him. There's one place I know where he might stand a chance.

Jez jumps down three steps at a time and swings round the bannister. 'C'mon little cuz, let's go.'

'Hang on,' I say. 'I've forgotten something.' I dash back into the garage and scoop Little Red into my school bag. I put the empty box outside, half hidden in the beech hedge.

Renée is waiting to wave us off.

'You're right about the pigeon,' I say. 'I've left him in a box beneath the hedge. Maybe he'll survive outside.'

I push past Jez, hugging my schoolbag against my chest. 'Come on. What are you waiting for?'

I climb on the school bus behind Jez. I don't want to sit with Tamsin and the others. I don't want them finding out what's in my bag. I smile at them and wave, but take an empty seat near the front.

'Budge up!'

I look up. Tamsin's come to join me. I look back down the aisle to see Erin glaring daggers at me. She usually sits next to Tamsin.

I slide my bag between my feet and hope Little Red

doesn't make a sound. 'How's Fish after Baba Yaga's chocolate curse?' I say.

'He's so mad at me,' grins Tamsin. 'But he thinks you're cool for going into Baba Yaga's.'

'You told him?' I say.

'Course I did. When we were little we used to peer in through her windows and run away. We dared each other to go in, but we never did.'

I smile. I think of telling Tamsin that's Baba Yaga's name is really Madame Popescu and that she doesn't steal children, but I don't want to spoil the story.

Tamsin opens a bag of crisps and offers me one. 'Dad says I can bring a friend to a match this weekend. Want to come?'

'Doesn't Erin want to go?'

Tamsin shrugs her shoulders. 'Dunno. Haven't asked.'

When the bus pulls up outside school, Erin shoves past me, swinging her bag in my face. I guess my novelty factor's worn off already. At least this gives me a chance to get away. I watch Erin, Tamsin and the others walk into school. Gracie looks back to find me in the crowd, but I hang back and lose myself behind some tall sixth-formers. I've got twenty minutes before registration, just time to get Little Red to safety.

*

I cross the road and slip away, weaving between the pupils on their way into school. I stop outside Madame Popescu's door and glance back at the school. I hope no one's seen me. I take a deep breath, knock, and let myself in.

I walk through the hall and find her in the kitchen.

Madame Popescu is filling the kettle with water. Fluffy slippers stick out beneath her dark green dressing gown. 'Scarlet, you've come back. I hoped you would. Maybe you'd like a biscuit and a cup of tea?'

I shake my head and fiddle with the straps on my bag. Maybe I shouldn't have come here. Maybe she doesn't need any more birds.

Madame Popescu frowns. 'Is there something wrong?'

'I need you,' I say. I feel tears pricking behind my eyes.

Madame Popescu puts down the kettle and walks towards me, head tilted on one side. 'How can I help you, child?'

I open my bag to show the scruffy pigeon sitting inside. 'His name's Red,' I say. I can't stop the tears from sliding down my face. 'I need you to help him fly.'

CHAPTER 17

I t's not until the end of the week that I get to visit Madame Popescu again. The teachers will be onto me if I miss any lessons and I haven't been able to go at lunchtimes because Tamsin and the others would see me leave school. Erin's blocked me out, and I don't know if she'd tell the teachers just to get me into trouble. But at least today Tamsin and the others are working over lunchtime to make costumes for a fashion show, so they won't see me slip away.

I knock on Madame Popescu's door and let myself in. She's sitting in her armchair listening to the radio. All the birds lift their heads to peer at me from their cages. Madame Popescu turns around.

'Scarlet, my dear! I wasn't expecting you. Why don't you put the kettle on and make us a nice cup of tea?'

In the kitchen, I fill the kettle, switch it on, and search for some teabags.

'You'll find them in the white jar.'

I turn around. I hadn't heard her walk in behind me.

She passes me the teapot. 'It might not look up to much. It's old and chipped, and stained with years of tea, but it still does the job,' she says. 'I was just about to make a cheese roll. Would you like one too?'

I nod and drop two teabags in the teapot.

She fixes me with her bright eyes. 'You'll be wanting to know about your bird.'

I search her face, looking for clues to how he is.

'Well, I won't lie to you,' she says. 'I didn't think he'd pull through. I had to put him under a heat lamp and give him lots of water. He had a nasty infection in his crop.'

'His crop?'

Madame Popescu touches the base of her neck. 'It's a pouch in his throat where he stores food before it goes into his stomach. His was too full, and the food had started to rot inside.'

I think about the bread that Jez and I forced down him and wonder if it was my fault.

'Will he get better?' I ask.

Madame Popescu squeezes my hand. 'He's a fighter,

that's for sure. With a bit of TLC, he should pull through.'

I frown. 'TLC?'

Madame Popescu smiles. 'Tender Loving Care. It makes a world of difference. Maybe one day we can set him free.'

I make the tea and pour it into two mugs; I place them on a tray with the cheese rolls and follow Madame Popescu into the sitting room.

'He's over there, in the end cage,' she says. 'Why don't you go and see him?'

I put the tray down on the low table. Crouching down at the end of the row of cages, I peer in at the little red pigeon.

Little Red is sitting at the far end of the cage, his rust-coloured feathers fluffed on his head. He presses himself against the farthest corner of the cage, his pink feet scrabbling against the floor as he tries to get as far away from me as possible.

'He's got his fight back in him,' I say.

'You can get him out,' says Madame Popescu. 'We need to clean him up a bit.'

I undo the catch and reach my arm in to grab him. I don't want to hurt him, so I hook my hand around him and slide him closer until I can wrap my hands around both wings.

'That's right,' says Madame Popescu, 'now hold him while I clean him up.'

I watch Madame Popescu wipe Red's beak and feet with a sponge, and I feel him relax beneath my fingers. Her hands are small and steady, and she doesn't stop until Red is clean again.

'There,' she says. 'All done. You can feed him while I clean out his cage.'

I sit with Red on my knees and watch him peck seeds from my hand. I can't believe how much he's changed in just four days. He's beginning to look like a proper pigeon now. His flight feathers have grown quite long, a mixture of white and rust red feathers. 'When can he fly?' I ask.

Madame Popescu is spreading clean newspaper in his cage. 'Well, he looks about three weeks old now. Pigeons usually leave the nest at about five weeks, but I think he'll be a bit later than that. When he's ready, we'll let him go.'

I don't want to think that far ahead. I want Red to see him before he goes. 'But how will he find his flock?'

Mrs Popescu puts her head on one side. 'They won't be too far away. I think we have to hope that they can find him.'

*

Scarlet Ibis

I sit with Madame Popescu until it's time to go back to school.

We eat cheese rolls and watch the news on TV. The birds peck at the food in their cages, a steady tap, tap, tap. Through the net curtains, I see people passing on the street and cars whizzing by. But it feels safe here, sealed off from the outside world. Madame Popescu doesn't probe me with loads of questions. She doesn't monitor my every move. She accepts me for who I am. She accepts me as me.

I look around the room to get clues about her, about who she is, but there are no books or photos or ornaments. Nothing at all, except for a silver cross on the mantelpiece and a plain clock on the wall. I don't feel like asking. Maybe she doesn't want anyone probing into her life either.

The hand on the clock points almost to the one. 'I'd better go,' I say.

She takes my plate from me, and smiles. 'Come back soon.'

Outside, the sun is bright. I shade my eyes and hurry back to school, just in time for geography. Erin's taken my seat next to Gracie. I don't want to sit next to Erin, so I sit further towards the front. But I can't concentrate in class at all. Red my brother and Little Red the bird get mixed up in my mind, like they're one and the same. Madame Popescu's voice is still whirling in my head and I can't untangle any of my thoughts at all.

I'm still thinking of Red when I get off the bus with Jez.

Back at the house, the Penguin's waiting for me in the kitchen. 'Hello Scarlet.'

I drop my school bag on the floor and look between Renée and the Penguin.

Renée puts her mug of tea on the table. 'Jo's come to talk to you about your mother.'

My heart thumps inside my chest. 'What's happened?'

Mrs Gideon smiles. 'Nothing, Scarlet. Come and sit down.'

I slide on to a seat, but don't take my eyes of her.

She leans forward. 'I just wondered if you would like to see your mother this weekend?'

I frown. 'Is she out of hospital?'

Mrs Gideon shakes her head. 'She's been moved to another unit, as she needs ongoing treatment, but we could arrange to meet up with her in a cafe, or somewhere like that.'

'OK,' I say. I wonder if we'll be left alone to talk, or if the Penguin will insist on listening in.

'Good,' says Mrs Gideon. Her smile is fixed on her face. 'Well, why don't I pick you up on Saturday at ten?'

Scarlet Ibis

'What about Red?' I say. 'Will he be there?'

She takes a deep breath in and breathes out slowly. 'Scarlet . . . ' she says, 'It's . . . '

' . . . complicated.' I finish for her.

'Scarlet, I'll be honest with you. I wish I could get things moving faster too. The review panel has had to postpone Red's case because of staff shortages. But we will take all your thoughts into consideration.'

I glare at her. 'Really?'

She leans forward. 'Really!'

'So let me see him,' I say.

She glances across at Renée, but Renée's staring into her cup. Neither of them can meet my eye. Then Mrs Gideon clears her throat. 'Scarlet . . . it's not for me to make that decision alone. He's settling in to his care home. It might upset him more if he sees you for just a short while.'

I slam my hands down on the table. 'At least tell me where he is.'

Mrs Gideon leans back in her chair and folds her arms. 'I can't do that, Scarlet.'

I push my chair back and leave the room. I run up the stairs, taking them two at a time, and slam my door. I slide down and press my back against it.

I don't know where Red is and, one thing's for sure,

the Penguin's not going to tell me. But I know Red needs me.

How can I hope to see my brother again if I don't even know where to look for him?

CHAPTER 18

I have to wait another two weeks before I see Mum. She's not been well enough, and each time she's cancelled at the last minute. I can hardly believe it when Mrs Gideon pulls up outside the house, ready to collect me.

Renée hands me the biscuits she helped me to make for Mum. I iced each one with a happy sunshine face. She squeezes my hand. 'See you later, Scarlet.'

I smile, and pack the biscuits in a bag along with the card I made for Mum. Mrs Gideon opens the car door for me, and soon we are driving towards the city. I'm on my way to see my mum.

I want to see her so much, but I've got butterflies in my stomach. It's been so long since I've seen her. Too long. I run my fingers down the beaded braids of my hair. Have I changed? Will Mum think that I have?

Mrs Gideon looks at me in the rear-view mirror. 'We're going to the zoo today.'

'The zoo?' I say.

'Your mother suggested it. We're meeting her there.'

I frown. The zoo is Red's and my place. Our special place. It won't feel right going there without him.

Mrs Gideon parks the car and we're queuing for the tickets when I feel arms around me.

'Scarlet!'

I turn round. 'Sita! What are you doing here?'

Sita smiles her big warm smile. 'Mum thought it might help if we came along too.'

I glance across and see my mum with Sita's. Mum looks somehow smaller than I remember. She's looking around, wide-eyed and nervous. She hasn't seen me yet. She looks like a lost child.

'We don't have to stay,' Sita says quickly. 'I mean, we can go off and leave you alone.'

'Please stay.' I say. I don't want to be alone with Mum today. Maybe I won't be able to think of anything to say to her. I take a step towards Mum. 'Hi,' I say.

Mum turns her head and looks at me. 'Scarlet!' she says.

Scarlet Ibis

Her mouth breaks into an unsteady smile. Maybe she's as nervous about this as me.

I fumble in my bag and pull out the biscuits and the card.

Mum takes them and just stares at them, as if she doesn't know what to do.

'They're lovely,' says Sita's mum. She opens the card and reads the words aloud for Mum to hear. 'Shall I hold onto them for now, and you can look at them later?'

Mum nods and lets her take them.

I take Mum's hands in mine. 'It's good to see you, Mum.'

Mum squeezes my hands. 'You too.'

We just stand there holding hands. Mum's hair's been cut into a bob, and it's curled and brushed so a hint of redness shines in the sunlight. I notice that her nails have been cut and polished. I wonder if Sita's mum has done this.

'Well, let's not just stand here getting cold,' says Mrs Gideon. 'Let's buy some tickets and go and see the animals.'

There's a long queue for the zoo. It snakes around the railings and is guided through a tent where a photographer is taking pictures of family groups against a green screen. On the advertisement board beside him are examples of family portraits where the green screen has been replaced by jungle, polar, and desert backgrounds. Sita and her Mum stand to have their photo taken. I don't want mine done, but the photographer takes a picture of Mum as she passes. She looks startled by the flash.

'Buy your photo on the way out,' he calls. 'Three for two.'

I frown at him, and move on through the ticket booth into the zoo.

I stick with Sita going around. Mum walks slowly, as if in a dream, not quite taking anything in. It's Sita's mum who's doing the talking, pointing things out, trying to get mum to smile.

It's only when we stop at the gorillas that Mum talks to me. She leans against the toughened glass and stares in at a huge gorilla grooming its small baby. 'Are they nice, the people looking after you?'

'They're fine,' I say. I don't want to say they're more than fine, because maybe Mum will think I want to be with them more than her.

We watch the baby gorilla climb down from its mother and explore a tree stump, working its fingers into the cracks. I read the information about the gorillas, how they live in large family groups in the wild, and forage in a wide area of jungle for food. I feel sorry for them cooped up here in the small enclosure.

Mum rests her head against the glass. 'I've not been much of a mum, have I?'

Scarlet Ibis

I slip my hand in hers. 'You're *my* mum,' I say. 'That's enough for me.'

Mum takes my hand and doesn't let go. 'I'm sorry, Scarlet.'

I lean into her. 'Don't be.'

'I'm trying, Scarlet, I really am.' She grips my hand even tighter. 'You're the reason that I'm here.'

'The Penguin says we can be in touch any time,' I smile.

Mum bites the corner of her lip. 'Once the flat has been done up, we'll be back there, Scarlet. I promise you. We'll get some nice things. Cushions and rugs, and pictures on the wall. We'll be together again. You'd like that, wouldn't you?'

I dig my hands deep in my pockets and force a smile. I wonder if Red is included this dream. She hasn't mentioned him at all. 'It'll be great, Mum,' I say, though I wonder if she's trying to convince herself as much as me. But I feel guilty deep down inside and wonder if Mum can read it in my face. The truth is, I don't want to live the way we lived before. I don't think I can. I want to live with Renée's family. I want Mum to live with them too. I want them to foster all of us. Mum and Red too. Mum needs to be looked after as much as me.

'Lunchtime,' announces Mrs Gideon.

I think she's on a tight time schedule, because we haven't seen much of the zoo yet and she keeps checking her watch.

She ushers us into the restaurant and plonks her bag on a table, taking out her purse. 'Why don't you take a seat here while I go and grab some drinks and sandwiches?'

I sit opposite Sita and we watch the Penguin join the food queue. Sita's mum and mine go off to find the toilets, leaving Sita and me alone.

'Thanks for coming,' I say.

Sita smiles. 'I miss you.'

'I miss you too.' I fiddle with a loose strap on the Penguin's bag. Even her bag annoys me. It's patent leather, black and white. It's probably stuffed with fish.

'Is it really OK where you are?'

I nod. 'It's fine, really. Well, it would be if Red was with me.'

Sita frowns. 'Don't you know where he is?'

I shake my head. 'Mrs Gideon says it takes time for the review panel to make their decisions. She says we might be better apart. Only she knows where Red is, and she's not going to tell me. I keep thinking of ways I could force her to tell. Maybe I could dangle her over the tigers, or throw her to the komodo dragons. Or maybe I could push her in with the giant spiders, or feed her to the lions.'

Sita smiles. She leans forward and whispers 'Maybe you could just look inside her bag.'

'What for?'

Scarlet Ibis

'Notes, papers . . . I don't know. Surely there'll be something with his address on.'

I just stare at Sita, and then at the bag between us on the table. 'Sita! You're a genius.'

Maybe I have the answer right in front of me.

I slide the zipper across, keeping my hand low on the table. I sift through magazines and a brochure for the zoo.

'Anything?' says Sita.

I shake my head. 'Nothing, just magazines, a few pens, and her phone.

Sita leans forward. 'Try her phone,' she whispers. 'Look at her emails.'

I turn it over in my hand. 'I don't know how to use it.'

'Give it here,' says Sita. She switches it on. 'Good job she's not bothered with a password.' She passes it to me. 'Scroll down the emails, like this. See if you find any about Red.'

I look up to see Mrs Gideon further along the queue. She's reached the self-service counter and I see her examining the sandwiches, turning a packet over in her hand. It's now or never. 'Keep an eye on her,' I say. 'Let me know when she's coming this way.'

I scroll down the list of emails. Some look work-related and others look personal. It's hard to tell them apart. I scroll down further and my heart skips a beat when I see a name.

Connor Mackenzie.

It's Red's official name, but I called him Red when he was born because of his mass of bright red hair, and the name just stuck. I click on the email and scan the page, but I can't see what I'm looking for.

'Scarlet! She's coming!'

I keep skimming down the page. His labels ping up in my face: Asperger's, autistic spectrum . . .

I glance up to see Mrs Gideon walking slowly, her eyes fixed on the tray, careful not to spill the drinks. I quickly flick down to the bottom of the email and find an address: *Meadowvale Children's Care Home.* I grab a pen and write the whole address on my arm.

'Scarlet . . . ' Sita hisses.

I slide the phone back into the bag just as Mrs Gideon looks up at us and smiles.

'Sorry for the wait, girls. Bit of a queue at the till.'

'Doesn't matter,' I say, pulling my sleeve over my arm.

'You girls,' she says, 'I expect you've not stopped chatting since I left you.'

I smile and look away, but I feel the writing tingle on my skin. I've got just what I need. I have the key to finding Red.

We eat our lunch while Sita's mum fills in the silent gaps. I can't think of what to say to Mum. I don't want to talk

about school or my new life with my foster family. I finish
my sandwich quickly and make my excuses to find the loo.
I just want some fresh air and to get away from the silence.
I'm walking across the lawns outside the restaurant when I
hear a man's voice shout my name.

'Scarlet!'

I turn. It's Jim, the Birdman.

'Hey, I thought it was you,' says Jim. He looks around.
'Where's your little brother?'

I swallow hard. 'Not here today,' I say. I force a smile and
run my fingers over the address written on my arm.

The Birdman frowns. 'Shame,' he says. 'I was hoping to
see him. I've got something for him. Maybe I can give it to
you to give to him instead?'

I nod. 'Of course.'

The Birdman points at the ground by my feet. 'Wait here
just a moment. Don't move. I won't be long.'

I wait in the middle of the lawn, rooted to the spot. I
watch children on the swings and slides behind the fence
of the play park. They look like another exhibit at the
zoo. I can't help thinking how weird humans are. Clothed
apes. That's all we are. Clever apes that have made cars and
aeroplanes and computers and concrete houses that reach
up into the sky; concrete houses which keep us apart.

Maybe life is better as a gorilla. Maybe it would be better to live in big family groups where everyone looks after everyone else.

'Hey!'

I turn around.

The Birdman is holding up a large brown envelope. 'I've been collecting them,' he says. He opens the envelope and I see it's packed full of feathers.

I pull out a scarlet ibis feather and hold it up to the light.

'Thought he'd like that one,' says Jim. 'It's his favourite, isn't it?'

I want to hug him, but I just smile instead. 'It's perfect.'

Jim turns to go. 'Get your brother to come next time. Tell him Woody's missing him.'

I stuff the envelope in my backpack and watch the Birdman walk away. I don't want anyone, especially the Penguin, seeing the feathers. They won't let Red have them. They don't understand.

Red might have lost his feathers in the fire, but I've got more for him. I've got another scarlet ibis feather, and I'm going to take it to him. I don't want him to think I've forgotten him.

I want Red to know I'm always here.

CHAPTER 19

I sit in the back seat of the Mrs Gideon's car as she drives me back. It was hard leaving Mum, but somehow even harder leaving Sita. Sita's mum said she'd look out for mine when she returns to the flat. She said she'd invite me round to stay some weekends too. When we said goodbye, Sita's mum handed me an envelope. She'd bought me the photo that was taken of Mum when we arrived. I wish I'd had my photo taken with Mum too, but at least I have a picture of her. It's the only one I have.

I lean against the window and watch as the roads pull us further away from the zoo and the city. Further away from Mum.

Mrs Gideon glances at me in the rear-view mirror. 'What were your favourite animals today?'

I shrug my shoulders. 'Don't know.'

Her eyes flick in the mirror to look at me again. 'Those biscuits that you made for your mum looked great. What did you put in them?'

'Stuff,' I say. I slump further back in the seat, out of her view. I know her tricks to try to get me to talk. If she wants to tell me something, she'll just have to say it right out. I fold my arms across my chest and stare out of the window, and wait.

'Scarlet.'

I hear the change in tone of her voice, more serious.

'Scarlet, your mother *is* getting better, but she may have to stay in hospital for some time.'

I say nothing.

'It may be that she will not be well enough to look after you, at all.'

I stare out at the blur of shops and houses. It's not as if this surprises me. I think I knew the moment I saw her looking lost and frightened at the zoo.

Mrs Gideon clears her throat. 'You'll still be able to see her. We can arrange regular meetings, if that's what you want.'

I take a deep breath and breathe out slowly.

'Scarlet, talk to me, love. I'm here to help. Are you OK?'

Scarlet Ibis

'I'm fine,' I say. 'Just fine.' The truth is, I don't know how I feel. I can't live with Mum. Maybe there's some relief, now that the decision has been taken from me. It's better than not knowing, being on the edge, neither one place nor the other. It's not up to me any more to make sure Mum is OK. I slide my sleeve back and look at the address written on my arm. 'What about my brother?' I say. It's the first time any of us has mentioned him today. 'Where will he live, if he can't live with me?'

'Once Red's needs are assessed we'll know.'

I fold my arms tight around me. No one tells me anything. It is worse not knowing, not knowing how he is.

But at least now I know *where* he is.

I know exactly where he is.

All I have to do now is find him.

After supper, I ask to borrow Renée's laptop to do some homework, but instead I look up the directions to Meadowvale Children's Home. I check on street view so that I can see the home, a large old house set behind metal fencing. I don't know if it's to keep the children in or to keep other people out. Shrubs and bushes on the other side of the fence screen the view of the front door. I try to memorize the houses and the street names. I write down my route to the home. I look up which buses and tube trains I need to get. It should take me about an hour to get there.

Renée puts her head around my door. 'Hi Scarlet! Can I come in?'

I exit the web page and turn over my page of directions.

She puts a mug on my desk and sits down next to me. 'Thought you might like a hot chocolate,' she says.

'Thanks,' I say. I close the laptop and fold my hands across it. I don't want more questions about Mum or being fostered.

Renée puts her head on her side. 'Jez and Theo are out tonight. I thought maybe you and I could have a girlie night; watch a DVD, share some popcorn?'

'Sounds fun,' I say. I try to smile. 'I'll be down in a minute.'

I wait until I hear Renée's footsteps on the stairs, then I slide the photo of Mum from the envelope. The green screen has been replaced by a polar background. Mum is standing on an iceberg, surrounded by penguins. She looks wide-eyed and afraid. I look into her eyes in the photo. It should be Mum and me watching a film tonight, like we used to do. It should be Mum and me cuddled up together on the sofa. But Mum stares back from her iceberg. It's as if

Scarlet Ibis

she's slowly drifting away, pulled by currents too strong for us, and there's nothing that either of us can do.

CHAPTER 20

By Monday morning I've made a plan. There's no way I could try to find Red at a weekend. Renée won't let me out for so long on my own, so I'll have to skip school instead. I sit on the school bus and clutch my bag to my chest. I double-check I have the twenty pound note from Renée safe in the zipper section. I'll need some money for the buses and the tube.

Tamsin squidges the bag with her fingers. 'What've you got in there?'

'Stuff for the fashion show,' I lie.

She frowns. 'You're not even in it.'

'I know,' I say. 'I've got some props for Mrs Adams.'

I hold the bag closer to me. Inside, I have spare clothes and the directions to Meadowvale, along with Red's new feathers.

Scarlet Ibis

I wait until after the first lesson, then tell Gracie that I have a dentist appointment and won't be back until the afternoon. We've double P.E. next, so I hope I won't be missed. I slip out to the playground, sling my bag up on the bike-shed roof, and scramble up the ladder. No one will see me here. I get changed into jeans and a sweatshirt, and pull a baseball cap low over my eyes. I grab the feathers and climb down from the bike shed, stuffing my schoolbag beneath the bike-racks, out of sight. I put my shoulders back and walk straight out of school.

No one tries to stop me. No one questions me on the tube. I try to tag along with someone, so it looks like I'm not on my own. When I leave the tube station I follow the roads to Meadowvale.

There are no meadows.

I pass a garage and shops and a launderette, and walk along a road lined with tall houses. Most of the houses have been turned into flats, the front gardens paved for cars instead of flowers.

The children's home has a large painted sign outside, with hills and a big happy sun. A high fence runs along the front of the house and continues along a side alley towards the back. I look at the buzzer and tannoy system on the

CHAPTER 20

entrance gate. It won't be easy to break in. Maybe Red isn't here at all. Maybe he's been moved on already.

I walk down the side alley and catch glimpses of a small garden area at the back of the building. Through the thick screen of shrubs, I can see bright plastic slides and swings. Some children are sitting at a table, wearing green aprons and spreading paint with their fingers. Children's laughter mixes with the sound of birdsong and traffic. I feel my heart thump in my chest. I want Red to be here, but I don't see him. Other children are spilling out from the house onto the small patch of lawn. Two women walk out to join them, mugs of coffee in hand, but I can't see Red anywhere.

I move further down the alleyway, spying through the bushes. Then I see him. I grip onto the wire fencing and try to pull a leafy branch out of the way to make sure it's him. But I am sure, even though his back is towards me.

I watch a lady in a flowery dress come towards him with a tray of drinks and biscuits. Red just sits, as if she's not even there. He's staring at the ground. She puts his drink and a biscuit beside him and walks away to find another child.

'Red,' I hiss.

He doesn't hear.

'Red,' I say a little louder. I don't want the staff to notice me.

Scarlet Ibis

Red swivels to look in my direction, but he can't see me yet, the thick shrubs screen me. I pull the scarlet ibis feather from the bag and push it through the wire, hoping he'll see a flash of red. It sails through the fencing and sticks out below the bottom of the hedge.

'Red!' I hiss again.

He stands up and begins to walk in my direction. He's seen the ibis feather. He picks it up and turns it over and over; whirling it in his hands, as if trying to make the connection. He looks different. His hair is cut short against his head and he's lost some weight.

'Red, it's me, Scarlet!'

That's when he sees me. He scrambles beneath the shrubs and presses himself against the wire, pushing his fingers through so that they can reach mine.

I curl my fingers into his. 'I'm here,' I say.

Red just stares at me, then starts pulling at the wire and kicking the base of the fence. 'Out . . . out . . . out!'

'Shh! Red.' I try to calm him, but he gets louder and louder, bashing the fence with his feet. Someone will hear him.

'Red!'

Flowery dress lady is standing in the garden, looking around, calling his name.

Red becomes more frantic. He pulls at the fence and a small corner comes away at the base. Before I can stop him, Red is on his tummy, scrambling beneath, the wire catching on his T-shirt, the gritty soil scraping his arms.

I pull him through and he presses himself as close against me as he can, as if he wants us to be one. He's moaning and crying.

'Shh! Red.' I stroke his hair, 'I'm here now. Shh!'

I don't think we can be seen behind the screen of leaves, but I can't keep Red quiet. Someone's going to hear him soon.

Someone's going to find us.

I can't just leave him here.

I don't even think about it.

I grab Red's hand,

and run.

CHAPTER 21

Red runs alongside me, one hand gripping mine, the other gripping the scarlet ibis feather. We don't stop until we reach the tube. I pull him in and we sit on empty seats at the far end of the carriage. I see people looking our way, and start to panic about whether we've been caught on CCTV. I pull the baseball cap further down over my face and lean into Red.

I squeeze his hand. 'You OK, Red?'

Red nods. He stares at the scarlet feather in his other hand. It's ragged where the barbs have come apart and he tries to smooth them together by stroking it along his sleeve.

'It'll be OK, Red.'

Red holds the feather up to his face and looks at me through the broken barbs. 'Are we going home?'

Such a simple question, but I don't know the answer. Home?

I don't know where home is.

I think of our flat, a burned shell. Even if it's been done up, we won't live there again. If I take Red to Renée's house, she'll call the penguins to take him away again. We have no home. Maybe we could try our luck on the streets. Kids do. Loads of kids do. If it was just me, I would. But it's not safe for Red, and that's all I want. I want him to be safe, and that leaves only one place I can think of.

Red tugs my arm. 'Where're we going, Scarlet?'

I smile, and whisper. 'We're going to see the birds.'

It's lunchtime by the time we reach Madame Popescu's house. I keep my head down as we pass the school gates and try to tag along behind a mother with a pushchair. I don't want anyone at school to see us. Madame Popescu's door is locked. I knock and knock. I hope she's not out, today of all days. I glance back at the school and see four figures on the bike shed roof. I tuck my head down and pull Red closer. I hope they haven't seen me. I don't think they'd even recognize me if they did.

When the door opens, I almost tumble through, pushing

Scarlet Ibis

Red ahead of me. Madame Popescu closes the door behind us.

I wrap my arms around Red. I lock my fingers into his. 'This is Red.'

I don't know what else to say. Where do I start?

Madame Popescu's eyes rest on Red for a while, and on the feather gripped in his hand. 'Hello Red,' she says. She looks between us and then shuffles past into the kitchen, nodding to herself as if she's been expecting him.

'I'll make some sandwiches,' she says. 'What would your brother like?'

I follow her into the kitchen. 'How did you know?'

She opens the fridge and looks in. 'Egg or cheese?'

I just stare at her. 'How did you know he's my brother?'

Madame Popescu chuckles. 'It's in the eyes.'

I frown. 'Mine are brown and his are blue.'

She puts the cheese on the table and walks right up to us. She's so small. Her eyes are level with mine. She looks right into me, and smiles. 'I see it in *your* eyes, Scarlet. He is everything to you.'

I grip Red tightly to stop my hands from shaking. Red clings on to me, but he doesn't take his eyes from Madame Popescu.

'I need you look after him, I say. 'I need you to keep Red safe.'

Madame Popescu puts her head on one side and looks at Red. She takes a deep breath in and lets it out slowly. 'Why don't you take Red to meet the birds, while I make us some lunch.'

'Come on, Red,' I say. 'Come and see the birds.'

I introduce him to Petre and Lukas and Anna-Maria. Red listens, silently mouthing their names.

'Madame Popescu looks after them all,' I say. 'She loves birds too. She keeps them safe.'

I kneel down by the end cage. 'There's someone you should meet.' I scoop the little red and white pigeon out and cup it in my hands. He looks like an adult pigeon now. His flight feathers are long and strong. He looks at Red with his bright pink eye.

'Know who this is?' I say.

Red frowns. He strokes the pigeon's soft chest feathers. I watch as his face lights up in recognition.

'Little Red,' he breathes. 'Really?'

I smile. 'It's him.'

A huge grin spreads across his face. 'He did it,' he says. 'I told him to fly, and he did.'

Scarlet Ibis

I frown. 'What d'you mean, Red?'

'The fire,' says Red. He grips my arm. 'His mother flew away so I pushed his nest off the ledge. I told him he had to fly too.'

'You pushed him off?' I say. *Red must fly, Red must fly.* Renée's words repeat over and over in my head. Now I know for sure Red wasn't trying to jump out of the window. He was just trying to save his little chick.

'Here,' I say. 'You hold him.'

Red cradles Little Red in his lap. I watch him run his hand from the pigeon's head to his tail feathers. Little Red becomes calm and turns his head to look at Red. Red touches the soft down of his chest. Red relaxes and I see his shoulders drop. He's happy just stroking the bird. I slump into the armchair. My head feels heavy. My whole body feels tired. All I want to do is to curl up and sleep, and sleep, and sleep.

Mrs Popescu shuffles in with a tray of sandwiches and three glasses of water. She places them on the low table. 'I made cheese,' she says, offering me a sandwich.

'Thank you,' I say. I take one and nibble at the corner. I feel too tired to eat.

Madame Popescu pulls up the footstool, sits on it, and watches Red.

'He's no trouble,' I say.

Madame Popescu nods her head. 'I can see that.'

'If you let him stroke the birds, he'll stay here all day.'

Madame Popescu raises one eyebrow. 'Is that what you want?'

I don't answer.

She leans closer. 'Do you want him to stay here all day? Every day?'

I close my eyes and put the sandwich back on the plate. I can't swallow. My mouth feels dry and my throat feels closed up inside.

Madame Popescu sweeps her hand across the cages. 'Do you want him to become like them?' Like Anna-Maria, or Petre, or Lukas?

I close my eyes and sink my head on to my chest. 'I don't know,' I say. 'I just want him to be safe.'

Madame Popescu gives a deep sigh. When I open my eyes, I see she is watching me.

'I don't know what else to do,' I say.

'He can stay,' she says, and pauses. 'He can stay, for now.'

I nod and blink tears away.

She sits and watches me, her hands pressed together beneath her chin.

Scarlet Ibis

The second hand on the clock goes round and round and round.

It's nearly half past two. I've just about got time to get to school, change into my uniform, and get to the last lesson.

I kneel down beside Red and pull out the envelope of feathers from the Birdman at the zoo. 'You've got to stay here for now, but I'll be back, Red, I promise you.'

Red keeps stroking Little Red.

'You're safe now, Red. I'll come back tomorrow, and the next day. I'll come every day. We're together now.'

I'm not sure Red even hears me. He's focused on the bird in his lap.

I crouch down next to him. 'I've got to go now, Red. Will you be OK?'

A smile spreads across his face. He pulls the pigeon to his chest and rests his cheek against its feathers. 'I'm Bird Boy now.'

CHAPTER 22

It's all over the breakfast news the next day.

**Boy, 8, missing from children's home.
Feared abducted.**

I feel sick as I watch the TV in the kitchen. Renée is clearing plates, not really listening. Jez is scribbling down some homework, but I can't help staring at the screen. A grainy CCTV image shows Red and me leaving the station. It just shows our backs. The newsreader says that the person with Red is a boy, a black youth in a hoodie and baseball cap. Red's description is given with no name. At least that gives me some time, but it won't be long before they work out it's me who took him. I'm already in trouble for missing classes yesterday. My form tutor wants to see me first thing today.

The Penguin hasn't even been round. Surely she should have told me by now that my own brother is missing. Maybe they want to keep me in the dark about that too.

'Hey Scarlet! You ready yet?'

I look across at Jez packing his homework away.

'I'll get my bag,' I say.

I rush up to my room and empty my school bag. I stuff in a couple of T-shirts and some leggings that might fit Red. I take a toothbrush and toothpaste from the bathroom for him too. I want to take some food from the kitchen, but Renée is still there clearing away, so I won't have chance. I just have to hope Madame Popescu can buy enough for Red.

On the bus I see Tamsin, Erin, Gracie, Laura, and Kim. None of them budge up for me to sit with them Tamsin glances up at me, but turns away tighter into the huddle. I move further down the bus and sit on an empty seat. I don't know what's up with them, but I'm glad they don't want me with them. I need time to see Red before the start of school.

I race along the road and let myself into Madame Popescu's house. She's with Red in the living room. Red's feeding Anna-Maria on his lap. He doesn't even seem to notice me when I sit next to him.

'You OK, Red?'

'Anna-Maria,' he says.

I stroke the soft feathers on her back. 'She's lovely, isn't she?'

Red points to all the birds and tells me their names, 'Petre, Lukas, Sergey, Elena, Victor . . . '

Madame Popescu shuffles across and sits on the footstool. 'He knows all their names already. And they know him.'

I watch Red, transfixed with Anna-Maria. Red feels safe here. Part of me wishes Madame Popescu could turn him into one of her birds, one of her children, and keep him here with her for ever.

My form tutor holds me back after registration.

'Scarlet, you weren't in maths yesterday afternoon.'

Inside I feel relieved. At least no one noticed I missed the whole of P.E. before lunch too. 'I didn't feel well,' I lie.

Miss P leans forward. 'I know things aren't easy for you, Scarlet, but you're a bright kid. You could do really well.'

I clasp my hands together and stare at them. I can feel Miss P's eyes on me.

'Is there anything you want to tell me?' she says.

I shake my head.

Scarlet Ibis

'Any friendship issues?'

I think of the way Tamsin and Erin and the others ignored me on the bus. It would be easy to say it's because of them, but I don't want to get them in trouble. I shake my head.

'Well,' says Miss P, 'if there's anything, anything at all, please come and talk to me.'

I nod, hoping her lecture's over.

She pushes back her chair. 'You can go now, but if you miss any more lessons, you know I will have to report it.'

I grab my bag and leave the room. Miss P hasn't the first idea what's going through my mind, and that's the way I want to keep it. But maybe it's the same for everyone, even her. Maybe we just don't know what battles other people are fighting.

In class, Erin and Gracie don't even look at me. They won't let me copy their work from yesterday's maths lesson. I don't know what I've said or done. Maybe Erin's convinced Tamsin I'm not worth talking to. I'm just not interesting to them any more. At lunchtime I grab a salad roll, crisps, and a flapjack from the canteen, and stuff them in my bag for Red.

I'm on my way out the door when Erin and Laura block my way.

Erin links her arm in mine. 'Tamsin wants to see you,' she says.

'I've got to go,' I say.

I feel Erin's arm grip harder. 'Tamsin wants to see you by the bike shed, now.'

I yank my arm away and shake her off. 'Let go of me.' A group of year nines on the table next to us have stopped eating and turn to look our way. Mrs Bentley's watching us too.

I pull my blazer straight and glare at Erin. 'I've got to go.'

Erin glares back. 'We know.'

I look between her and Laura.

Laura leans forward. 'We know. We saw you yesterday.'

My mouth goes dry. I clutch my bag tighter to my chest.

Erin pokes her finger against my bag crunching the crisp packet inside. 'You wouldn't be saving food for anyone, would you?'

I feel my heart thumping against my chest. They did see me yesterday. How could I have been so stupid to walk past the school at lunchtime? 'Don't tell,' I say.

Erin links her arm in mine again. 'You'd better come and see Tamsin.'

I'm marched across to the bike shed. A cold wind is blowing, tugging at my skirt and blazer. Above, the clouds are heavy, pressing down, threatening rain. Tamsin, Gracie, and Kim are huddled beneath the bike shed, sitting on the rails of the bike racks.

Waiting.

They form a circle around me. Only Gracie gives me a fleeting smile.

Rain begins to patter on the tin roof above our heads.

Tamsin stands up and looks me up and down. 'We saw you yesterday. We saw you with that boy, the one that's been on the news.'

I look at each one of them. They must've seen us when we entered Madame Popescu's house.

Tamsin doesn't take her eyes from me. 'What does Baba Yaga pay you?'

I frown. 'Pay me?'

'What does she pay you to find children for her?'

I want to laugh. 'Are you serious?'

Erin leans forward. Her eyes are narrow, her mouth a thin hard line. 'You told us yourself that you'd find more children for her.'

'You're crazy, all of you,' I say. I try to step out of the circle but they close around me. I can tell from their faces it's me who they think's crazy.

Tamsin grabs the edge of my blazer. 'A boy was abducted yesterday and we saw you with him.' She pulls her phone from her pocket and zooms into the image on the screen. It shows a blurred picture of Red and me standing outside Madame Popescu's house. 'How d'you explain that?'

Rain falls harder. It drums on the tin roof and falls in sheets on to the concrete, sealing us inside the bike shed.

Tamsin's still waiting for an answer. Her face is close to mine. I lean even closer so our noses are almost touching. I speak through gritted teeth. 'It's none of your damn business.' I look around them all. 'It's nothing to do with any of you.' I push past Tamsin and walk out into the rain.

Tamsin's voice calls after me. 'The police will want to know.'

I stop dead and turn around.

'That's right, you heard me.' She just stands there, hands on hips, challenging me. 'Reckon you could go to prison. You and that witch, Baba Yaga. You're in it together.'

The rain falls harder. It runs down my face and around my neck, beneath my collar. I feel it soak through my skirt against my skin. 'Madame Popescu,' I say. 'Her name is Madame Popescu. She's not a witch.'

'Witch or no witch,' Tamsin says, 'you and her have taken a child.'

Scarlet Ibis

I see them watching me from the safety of their shelter, screened behind a sheet of rain.

'He's my brother,' I say. 'My brother, Red.'

Tamsin looks around the others and laughs. 'Your brother? Really?' The corner of her mouth curls in a smirk on her face. 'You expect us to believe that?'

I wipe the rain from my eyes, stand up tall, and face them. 'Yes,' I say. 'No one must know. No one must know, or they'll take him away from me.'

Tamsin folds her arms and stares at me. 'So how come you haven't mentioned him before? How come he's not living with you at Jez's, too?

I take a deep breath. 'I'm not Jez's cousin,' I say.

I see the others glance at each other and hear Erin mutter '*I told you so.*'

'My mum's not got cancer. But she's ill. She can't look after us any more. So Red and me, we're in care.'

Tamsin's about to say something, but she hesitates, her mouth open as if the words have stuck in her throat. Erin and Laura shift on their feet and glance at each other.

I take a step towards them. 'It's all right for you,' I say. 'You can go back to your nice homes with your nice families. You can have your meals cooked every night. Your mums and dads look after you. They're not crazy.

They don't swear at you or call you names. But Red and I don't have that. We don't have anything like that. All we've got is each other. And if you tell on us, we'll be split up, and then we won't have anything at all.'

CHAPTER 23

I spend the rest of lunchtime with Red and Madame Popescu. I imagine the teachers and penguins crashing into the house and hauling Red away.

But it docsn't happen. Instead, I sit with Red at the kitchen table while he paints red handprint birds on a roll of old blue wallpaper.

I watch him dip his hand into the paint and press it carefully against the textured paper.

'Caroni Swamp,' he says, and smiles.

I dip my hand in the paint and press my handprint next to his. It overlaps, our fingertips touching, like the wingtips of scarlet ibis in flight.

We sit in silence and print more birds, a huge flock across the whole piece of paper, blocking out the sky.

Madame Popescu shuffles through and sits with us. Little Red is cradled in her hands. 'He's doing well,' she says.

I look across at the pigeon. He's lost his frightened look and sits calmly in her hands. All his adult feathers are through. His white and rust-red feathers look sleek and healthy. His bright eyes watch the patch of sky through the window.

Madame Popescu runs a finger across his wings. 'He's stronger than you think,' she says. She glances across at Red, and then at me. 'I can't keep him here for ever. You know that, don't you? It wouldn't be fair.'

'He's not ready,' I say.

Madame Popescu sighs. 'I cannot keep him here, much as I would love to. I am just an old, old woman. He needs his family.'

I notice Red's hands have paused, hovering above the painted birds.

I swallow hard. 'But he'll be lost. How will his family find him again?'

Madame Popescu tucks the pigeon under her arm and takes a handful of seed. 'Come with me,' she says.

Red and I follow her out on to the small courtyard patio. The paving slabs are dark from the recent rain.

'What do you see?' she says.

Scarlet Ibis

I look around. Madame Popescu's house backs on to
other houses. The sky-space above us is small, a square of
white cloud above. 'I see nothing,' I say.

Madame Popescu chuckles. 'Then look again.' She
scatters her handful of seed across the ground, and suddenly
the air is filled with beating wings. I see the birds coming
from above, from window ledges and rooftops. They flutter
down and peck around our feet for fallen seeds. Little Red
struggles in her hands to join them.

Madame Popescu smiles. 'You see, they came.' She strokes
Little Red's chest. 'They are out there, and I will help,' she
says. 'I will help Red to find where he belongs. I will help
him to find his family.'

Mrs Gideon's waiting for me when I get back from school.
She turns to me as I step into the kitchen. Renée's face is
long and serious with concern. The Penguin puts her phone
down on the table. Do they know I was the one who took
Red? There are no police here to take me away, so I guess
they haven't worked it out yet.

'Sit down, Scarlet,' says Mrs Gideon.

I take a seat, and stare at the table in front of me,
concentrating on the knots in the wood.

Mrs Gideon sits down beside me. 'We have some upsetting news. Your brother is missing.'

I feel blood rush to my head and grip my hands tightly together.

'We are doing everything we can to find him.'

I take a deep breath and pretend to be shocked and scared. I grab my bag and turn to Mrs Gideon. 'You promised me you could keep him safe,' I yell. 'But you couldn't even get that right.'

I storm upstairs. It was a mean thing to say, but I don't care. They've kept me in the dark for so long maybe it's my turn to keep them in the dark now.

I empty my bag on the bed. One thing's clear; I can't stay here. Red and I will have to move on. Maybe we could get to Trinidad, but neither of us have a passport. We'll just have to chance it on the streets. There was a programme on TV about street kids looking after each other. We could join them, and get by somehow. I start filling my school bag with clothes and roll up a blanket to put in there too. It might be cold, but at least Red and I will be together. We'd keep each other warm. It's a plan, a scary plan, but at least I'm doing something. It's the endless waiting, waiting, waiting that I can't stand. Something has to happen. I have to make it happen. Tomorrow night, we'll be somewhere else. I don't know where, but at least Red and I will be together.

I stuff my bag at the end of the bed when I hear a knock at the door. Jez comes in and sits down on the bed beside me.

He's shaking his head. 'Sorry to hear about your brother, Scarlet.'

I stare at my hands. I don't want to lie to Jez.

Jez puts his arm around my shoulder. 'We'll help you find him.'

I nod.

'We all want to help.'

I grip my hands tightly together. 'Thanks.'

Jez gets up and paces to the window. 'Look Scarlet,' he says. 'I'm sorry if I gave you a hard time when you came here.'

'You didn't,' I say. 'It's OK here. Really.' I fiddle with a loose thread on my sleeve. 'Your mum and dad have been good too,' I say. I look up at him. 'Make sure you thank them from me, won't you?'

Jez frowns. I don't know if he's seen my bag packed at the end of the bed. I hope I haven't made it obvious that I'm leaving.

'We'll find him for you, Scarlet,' says Jez. 'We won't stop until we do.'

*

The next morning, I leave the house with Jez. It's my last time here. I know I'll miss it. Maybe it was the closest I'll ever get to having a family; feeling like I belong. I want to put my arms around Renée and thank her for looking after me. I don't want her to get in trouble because of me.

On the school bus, Tamsin puts her P.E. bag on the floor to give me space to sit down. She watches me closely. I don't want to talk about Red or ask if she's called the police.

I stare at her bag on the floor. 'Didn't know we had P.E. today.'

'It's for Friday. Mum washed it for me.'

'Oh,' I say. I hold my own bag on my lap and feel the bulge of clothes and the blanket squashed inside. I run through my escape plan. Go to registration, geography, and then English, because Mrs Cooke follows up all absences. Then, at break, slip out to Madame Popescu's and take Red. I'll tell Madame Popescu our mum wants us back home. I'll tell her it's all OK.

I don't even notice the bus has pulled up outside school. Tamsin gives me a shove and I clamber out with everyone else. I feel different somehow. No one knows that after break I'll be gone. I feel like I'm floating, suspended. Everyone's lives will carry on with the routine of school, but I'll be somewhere else.

Tamsin grabs my arm. 'We want to show you something,' she says.

I look around. Gracie, Erin, Laura, and Kim have formed a circle around me. I don't want more questions. 'What?' I scowl.

Tamsin pulls me with her. 'Not here,' she says.

I'm half marched with them to the bike sheds. Tamsin slings her P.E. bag on the floor and it lands with a heavy clunk. I can hear metal crunch against metal inside.

'What's in there?' I say.

Tamsin looks between Gracie and Erin 'You're not Jez's cousin. I got Fish to ask Jez himself. You and your brother are in care. We believe you.'

I frown, and take a back step from them.

'So we know you're telling the truth,' says Erin. 'That's your little brother in Baba Yaga's house.'

'Madame Popescu's,' I say. I don't know where this conversation's going. I want to leave with Red before anyone finds out.

Tamsin reaches down and unzips her bag. 'We reckon you're telling the truth about him being taken away,' she says.

I narrow my eyes. 'You do?'

Tamsin nods and points down at her open bag. 'Reckon you might need these.'

I stare into the bag. It's filled with tins of food, packets of crackers and biscuits, and a couple of frozen pies.

'I got them from my dad's shop. They're out of date so he'll only throw them away'

'I can get you some clothes my brother's grown out of,' says Gracie.

Erin nods. 'We could take turns teaching him.'

'Yeah,' Laura says. 'We could take him to the park and cinema and stuff.'

Tamsin grins. 'He's like our secret. Our secret little brother. What d'you reckon, Scarlet?'

I frown. 'Why would you want to do that?'

Gracie fumbles with her bag. 'If my brother was taken away, I'd do anything to get him back.'

I look around them all.

Tamsin puts her hands on her hips. 'We're your friends aren't we, Scarlet? What else are friends for?'

All through geography my head is scrambled. Could it work, would it work? Could we really keep him secret? He'd be safe with Madame Popescu. Safer than on the streets, that's

Scarlet Ibis

for sure. I climb the stairs to English. I'll have to make a decision soon. Do I stay or do I go? I slide along the seats and sit down at my place by the window. I look along the street to Madame Popescu's house.

The trees are coming into bud. Everything looks bright and green and fills me with a sense of hope. But then, I see them. I grip on to the table and feel sick deep down inside. Two police cars are pulled up outside Madame Popescu's house, and I recognize the Penguin's red car too.

I push my chair back and start running out of class.

But it's too late. I know that, even now. I can't save Red. By the time I get there Red will have gone.

Red will be taken away from me for good this time.

And there won't be anything I can do.

CHAPTER 24

I run out of school. I hear the receptionist calling me, but I don't stop. I run and run, but I'm in a nightmare dream of running and I can't get there fast enough. I see the Penguin's car pull out and drive away. I'm too late. She's got Red, I'm sure of that.

I stop outside the house and watch her car disappear into the traffic.

'Scarlet? Scarlet Mackenzie?'

I turn and see a police officer walking towards me from Madame Popescu's house. I try to look beyond her to see if Madame Popescu is inside.

'Scarlet, we need you to come with us.'

'I want to see Madame Popescu,' I say. I push past her into the hallway. Madame Popescu is sitting in the kitchen, her hands folded on the table. The police officer sitting next to her has his notebook out beside him.

'Where's Red?' I say.

Madame Popescu sits back in her chair. She looks tired and old. She's lost the twinkle in her eye. 'They have taken him, for now,' she says.

I ignore the police officer taking notes. 'But how did they know? How did they find out?'

Madame Popescu sighs. 'Scarlet, I had no choice. I had to tell them.'

I just stare at her. 'You? I trusted you.'

'Scarlet, listen . . .'

I back away from her. 'You said you'd help. You said you'd keep him safe.'

'Scarlet . . .'

I turn away and walk through the hall, kicking at piles of newspaper. I clench my fists so hard I feel my nails dig in my skin. No one ever listens. No one listens to what I have to say.

I think the police will take me to the station and lock me in a cell, but instead they take me back to Renée's.

I storm upstairs, fling myself in bed, and pull the covers

over me. I hear Renée come into the room and sit next to me on the bed.

She tries to talk to me, but I pull the covers tighter round me.

I don't want to be here at all. I want to be with my own mum. I want Mum so much it hurts. I remember when I was little how she used to pick me up when I fell over and she'd hold me tight until the pain had gone away. I want to go back to that time. I want it to be how it was, before everything got complicated. I want it to be how it was when everything seemed OK.

I must have fallen asleep eventually, because when I wake the morning sun is streaming through the window. I glance at the clock. 10.30 a.m. I've slept right through one day and into the next. I've missed school. I sit up and rub my eyes. My head hurts and my whole body aches. A chocolate bar and a piece of paper lie on my desk. I pick up the note and read it. *We'll still help you find him. Jez X*

I pull a dressing gown around me, even though I'm still in school uniform, and make my way down the stairs.

Theo is sitting at the kitchen table tapping on his laptop. He folds it closed and leans back in his seat when I come in.

Scarlet Ibis

'Hi, Scarlet. D'you want some breakfast?'

I look through to the living room. 'Where's Renée?'

'She's gone to the review panel with Jo.'

'About Red?' I say.

Theo nods. He gets up and puts the kettle on. He opens a packet of bread. 'Toast?'

I nod, and slide along to sit on one of the chairs. 'What's going to happen?'

Theo puts the bread in the toaster. 'I don't know. That's what we'll find out today.'

I stare down at my hands. If Madame Popescu hadn't called social services, Red and I would have been far away today. 'I'm in trouble, aren't I?'

'You're not in trouble, Scarlet.' Theo waits for the toast to pop up. He brings it over to the table with the butter and jam. 'Jez wanted to stay home and keep you company today.'

I manage a smile. I think of the chocolate he left for me in my room. I spread the butter and spoon a lump of jam onto the toast. 'I can't stay here, though, can I? Not after yesterday.'

Theo sits down next to me. 'Do you want to stay with us?'

I take a bit of toast and chew it slowly, but I don't say anything. I don't know what I want, any more.

*

I try to do some homework, but I can't concentrate, so I end up watching TV instead. Renée still hasn't returned. The hands on the clock move round so slowly, from twelve to one, to two, to three o'clock. I can tell Theo is impatient too. I hear him pacing upstairs, but he can't settle and he joins me watching TV. I see him check his phone. I don't know what can be taking them so long.

It's nearly four o'clock when Renée and the Penguin arrive back at the house. Renée's face is strained. She ushers the Penguin into the kitchen and boils the kettle for a cup of tea. The Penguin puts her bag on the table and sits down at the far end. I see Renée and Theo exchange glances. Renée kicks off her shoes and slumps down in a chair next to the Penguin. She presses her fingers to her forehead and closes her eyes. Theo puts the cups of tea on the table and sits with his back to me, so that I can't see either of their faces.

'Well?' I say.

Renée looks up at me. Her face looks drawn and tired. 'Scarlet, give me a few minutes please. I need to talk with Theo.'

I go back into the sitting room, curl up on the sofa in front of the TV, and turn the sound up high. Renée's exhausted.

Scarlet Ibis

She doesn't want to talk. It's useless asking, anyhow. No one tells me anything. I'm used to it now.

I watch back-to-back cartoons. I flick through the channels and watch shiny people selling shiny jewellery. Jez comes home and I hear him talking to his parents in the kitchen. I mute the sound and listen to snatches of conversation. My name is mentioned. It seems unfair that they are talking to Jez without talking to me first. I turn the sound up and ignore him when he sits next to me, munching a bag of crisps. He grabs the remote and turns the sound off.

'You OK, little cousin?'

I just stare at the silent screen.

'Tamsin and the others were asking after you today.'

I don't feel like talking so I try and grab the remote, but Jez holds it out of reach.

'How come you never told me about your brother when you first came here?'

I sit back and fold my arms across my chest. 'How come you never asked?'

Jez shrugs his shoulders. 'Good point, I guess.'

'Put the TV back on?' I say.

'Mum and Dad want to see you.'

'Me?' I say.

'Yes, you,' says Jez. He flicks the TV off and gives me a

shove. 'Come on.' He hauls me up and I follow him into the kitchen.

Renée looks tired, but she pats the chair next to her and smiles at me. I sit down between her and Theo, while Jez leans against the sink stuffing bread into his mouth.

Mrs Gideon shuffles papers on the table. She looks at me over half-moon glasses. 'We had a very long meeting about Red today.'

I search her face for clues, but can't tell what she's about to say.

'It hasn't been an easy decision to reach,' she says. She pauses. 'We want to do what's best, but it's . . . '

' . . . complicated.' I finish her sentence. I yawn. I've heard all this before.

'But,' she says, and looks at Renée and Theo, 'it has been decided that if Renée does specialist training, then Red might be able to come and live here with you too.'

'Here?' I say. I can barely speak.

Renée smiles and nods.

'With me? Here, together?'

Mrs Gideon leans back in her chair. 'Renée will need to enroll for the training, and there will be plenty of checks, but the review panel decided that Red will thrive and learn best with you around, in a family situation.'

Scarlet Ibis

Renée takes my hands in hers. 'If all goes well, he could be with us in the next few days.'

I look between them all. Jez has a big grin on his face. Renée and Theo are smiling too.

'What happened in the meeting?' I say.

Renée leans forward, so her voice is almost a whisper. 'Madame Popescu,' she says. She squeezes my hands tight, and I see tears brim in her eyes. 'Madame Popescu came to the meeting. She told us a story, a story that changed everybody's minds.'

Chapter 25

I help Jez and Theo clear the books and computer stuff from the small study. Theo and Renée have made a new office space in their bedroom so that Red can have a small room of his own. Avril's back for the weekend, and she helps decorate Red's room too. We paint the walls dusk blue and Renée lets me choose a dark green rug for the floor. I stand on Red's new cabin bed and hang a bird mobile of scarlet ibis from the ceiling. Avril helped me make the birds from dyed feathers and red felt.

I fluff up Red's pillow and lay his feathers out on the duvet, placing the scarlet ibis feather on his pyjamas. Red will be safe here.

'Hey, Scarlet!' Avril puts her head around the door, a huge grin across her face. 'Someone's here to see you.'

Scarlet Ibis

Red slides into the room. He just stops and stares at me, and then at the feathers. I pick up the scarlet ibis feather and wrap my arms around him. He puts his arms around my waist and hugs me so tightly I can barely breathe.

Avril smiles. 'Come down when you're ready. We're having pizza tonight.'

I sit with Red on his bed and we lay the feathers out in a row: Amazilia hummingbird, Bali starling, blackbird, blue-winged kookaburra, honeycreeper . . . He knows them all. Red makes sure each feather is smoothed straight so they catch the sunlight and shine, some iridescent.

I lie on my back and look up at the scarlet ibis mobile. The breeze from the open window turns the birds round and round and round. The flock of ibis flies against a dusky sky.

Red lies back next to me and pushes his hand into mine. 'Tell me a story, Scarlet.'

'Later,' I say. The smell of pizza drifts up into the room. 'Come on, Red. Time to eat.'

Red follows me downstairs. He leans into me when everyone turns to look at us.

'We're having a TV supper tonight,' says Renée.

I'm pleased because it will take the focus off Red.

'Hey, Red,' says Jez. 'He crouches down next to Red. 'We got you a welcome present.'

Red keeps his eyes on the floor and takes the package from Jez's hands. He pushes it towards me. I crouch down too. 'Let's see, Red. Let's see what it is.' I peel back the wrapping and pull out a DVD.

'Look, Red,' I say. '*The Life of Birds*. Looks great, doesn't it?'

Red takes the DVD and turns it over and over, staring at the pictures of birds. He pushes it back into Jez's hand.

Jez looks hurt. 'Doesn't he like it?'

I smile. 'He wants you to put it on.'

'Now?' says Jez. His eyebrows shoot up his forehead. 'It's just that I was going out to meet Fish.'

Renée smiles. 'I'm sure Fish won't mind waiting. '

Jez shrugs his shoulders. 'Um, fine. Sure thing.'

Red takes Jez by the hand and they walk into the sitting room. There's something about Jez that makes anyone feel safe. Red feels it too.

I'm helping Renée cut the pizza and put salad in a bowl, when there's a knock at the door and Mrs Gideon arrives. She's wearing jeans and a flowery top. I guess she's not on duty now.

Renée asks her to join us for pizza.

'Thanks, but I can't stay.' She says. 'I just thought I'd drop in to check everything's OK. I was just passing through.'

Scarlet Ibis

I frown. I didn't think Mrs Gideon lived near here. I guess she's come out of her way just to see us.

'Red's fine,' I say.

'Good,' she says. She just stands there, as if she doesn't quite know what to do or say. 'Good. Well, it's times like this that remind me why I do my job.'

I step forward, put my arms around her shoulders and hug her. 'Thank you, Jo,' I say. 'Thank you for listening.'

She pulls a tissue from her pocket. 'I'd better go before I make a fool of myself,' she says. 'But Scarlet . . . '

I look at her and smile.

' . . . you take good care of him.'

'I will,' I say. 'I will.'

I carry pizza into the sitting room for the others.

Red's sandwiched between Jez and Theo, his eyes fixed on the TV, watching all the different birds.

Renée sits down next to me, and smiles.

What was Madame Popescu's story?' I ask. 'What did she say that made the difference?'

Renée wraps her arm around me. 'She told us the story about her birds.'

'Her birds? What have they got to do with Red?'

Renée smiles. 'Everything. I think I should let Madame Popescu tell you that story herself.'

CHAPTER 26

'Zoo day tomorrow, Red,' I say.

Red nods and runs ahead of me, hopscotching across the paving stones.

Tomorrow we'll see Mum too. We'll walk around the zoo, look at the animals, and eat ice cream.

We'll be just like any other family.

Because that's exactly what we are.

Family.

We might not be perfect; maybe there is no perfect family. But we have each other, and that's what counts. I used to think that Mum didn't want us. I used to think that maybe she didn't even love us. But I know that's not true. Mum writes me letters now. She tells me more in those letters than she's told me in years. Mum loves us. I know that now. She lives for us.

We are the sunshine in her darkness.

But Red and I have another family. Renée is like a mother hen, lifting her wings and taking us in. She's training to look after Red and understand his needs. Theo's even trying to convince Renée to get some chickens for the garden, so Red can look after them. Jez, Avril, and Nan have scooped us in, as if we've always been here.

I push my hands deep in my pockets and follow Red. He's waiting for me at the street corner in the dappled shadow of a tree. The new leaves are small and bright green, backlit by sunlight. Red's hopping from foot to foot, impatient to be off. He grabs my hand and pulls me along with him.

I trot alongside him to keep up. 'Who're we going to see today?'

'Poppy,' he says, a big grin spreading across his face.

I smile, because Red doesn't call Madame Popescu by her full name. He just calls her Poppy.

'And who else?' I say.

'Petre,' Red says, ' . . . and Anna-Maria and Lukas and Elena and Sergey and Victor . . . '

'Who else?' I know who he wants to see most of all.

'Little Red,' he shouts.

'I want to see him too,' I say.

Scarlet Ibis

We pass my school. The lights are out. The playground is empty. It's shut and sleeping on a Saturday.

'Nearly there,' I say.

Sunlight bounces from the bonnets of cars, glaring in our eyes.

Red and I are running now. The pavement blurs beneath our feet.

It's only as we reach Madame Popescu's that I notice the small crowd gathered around her house. A white van is parked up outside, its wheels half on the pavement.

I grab Red and pull him to a stop. The doors at the back of the van are open and I see cages piled inside. I see Petre, Lukas, and Elena. Petre is mewling, clattering his beak against the bars. I can see the fear in his eyes. A man in white overalls walks from the house, a cage in his arms. Inside the cage I see Anna-Maria, white feathers fluffed and pressed against the wire.

I push my way through the people and grab on to the cage. 'What are you doing?'

The man pulls the cage away from me and pushes it into the van. 'Hey, don't touch, they're not clean.'

I try to look inside to find Little Red, but the man slams the van doors closed.

'You can't take them,' I say.

The man ignores me and climbs into the driver's seat.

A man with a camera is snapping pictures of the house.

My heart is thumping deep inside. If I hadn't taken Red to Madame Popescu's, no one would have found out about her birds. It's our fault they're being taken away from her.

I bash on the side of the van. 'Wait,' I yell.'

I'm brushed aside. Another man in overalls climbs into the front of the van. The engine revs and smoke puffs from the exhaust.

I feel Red's hand grip mine.

'WAIT!' I yell. 'WAIT!'

But I can't stop them. The orange indicator light flashes and the van pulls out into the traffic, taking Madame Popescu's birds away.

I turn and push my way through the crowd of people, through the mutterings . . .

Mad.

Disgusting.

Filthy.

Cruelty case.

Shouldn't be allowed . . .

Madame Popescu's front door is still open. I pull Red through and shut the door, hearing the click of the lock, and I slide the chain across.

Scarlet Ibis

'Madame Popescu?' I shout.

I open the door to the living room, but it's now an empty space. Golden specks of dust, and feathers hang suspended in mid-air. There is nothing left in here. All the birds are gone.

I pull Red into the kitchen and see Madame Popescu through the window. She's sitting on a bench in the garden, rocking slowly backwards and forwards. A small box is balanced on her knee. I pull Red with me and crouch down beside her.

'Madame Popescu?' I say. I look up at her. Tears course down the deep lines in her face and mark the cardboard box with dark droplets. She doesn't seem to realize we are here.

Red sits down next to her.

I put my hand on hers. 'Madame Popescu. It's me, Scarlet. It's me and Red.'

Madame Popescu grips my hand. 'They took them away,' she says. 'They took all my little children.'

'We'll get them back,' I say.

Madame Popescu's hands are trembling, but she is looking beyond me to somewhere I can't see. 'They came and took them away. They took Petre with his bad leg and Lukas who had been left for dead down by the river. They took Elena and Victor, Magda and Sergey, Marius and Erik.'

She closes her eyes and a sob racks through her body. 'They took sweet little Anna-Maria too. All my beautiful children. Gone.'

'I'm so sorry,' I say. I don't know what to do. Madame Popescu looks smaller somehow, and older.

She opens her eyes and wipes the tears with a ragged handkerchief. 'Many, many years have passed, yet in my heart it still feels like yesterday.'

'Many years?' I feel an ache deep down in my chest, because now I understand. Now I know Madame Popescu is not talking about the birds. This is Madame Popescu's story.

'I took them in because no one wanted them,' she says. 'I took them in because they needed family. They needed love. My wonderful children. My little Petre, so spirited. My serious Lukas. My beautiful Anna-Maria. She couldn't walk or talk, but she was full of love.'

'When was this?' I say.

Madame Popescu holds both my hands so tightly that it almost hurts. 'Once upon a time, I lived in a house on the edge of a village, surrounded by fields and woodlands. My husband was a doctor, and although we were very happy, our only sadness was that we could have no children of our own. We prayed for children, and our prayers were answered the day my husband brought Petre home. He was young boy, only two years old. He had been injured in a farming accident and his parents could not afford to keep him, so we took him in.' Madame Popescu smiles. 'Of course, Petre was not the only one. Soon many came to join us. Some were even left on our doorstep without a note to tell us their names.'

'But what happened?'

Madame Popescu shakes her head. 'My country was going through dark times. Our people were divided. We were not free. We were not free to think or dream. But my husband spoke out against the leaders of the country. He wanted food and medicine for the people.' She touches her finger to the cross around her neck. 'And one night, the police came and took us from our homes, and from each other. There was nothing I could do. I never saw them again.'

I put my arm around her.

'All gone. I couldn't save them,' she says. 'They took all my little children.'

I sit with her in silence, and watch the cloud shadows race across the ground.

Madame Popescu reaches into her pocket and scatters seed on to the patio. Pigeons begin to spiral from the sky.

Down they come, whirling around us, the air singing with their wing-beats. They strut around our feet, pecking at the seeds on the ground.

She looks up and smiles through her tears. She ruffles Red's hair. 'But we saved one, didn't we.'

I look across at Red. His eyes are fixed on the cardboard box on her lap. I can hear the scrabble of claws inside.

Madame Popescu fumbles with the lid of the box. 'Help me with this,' she says.

Red and I take a corner, and with Madame Popescu we pull the cardboard flaps open wide.

Little Red tip taps inside and cocks his head upwards. He looks up at the birds above him, framed against a patch of sky.

Red reaches in and wraps his hands around the pigeon's wings.

Madame Popescu watches him and smiles. 'It's time,' she says.

Red stands among the other pigeons and throws Little Red into the air. He lifts upwards, in a blur of feathers. The other pigeons explode into the sky too. I feel the blast of air from beating wings.

I take Madame Popescu's hand and hold it tight.

'You saved him.' I say.

Scarlet Ibis

We watch our little pigeon swirl with the flock, protected by the other birds. Round and round he flies, higher and higher, up into the clear blue sky.

'You saved him, 'I say. 'You are the one who helped him fly.'

Epilogue

'Be careful, Red,' I say.

He looks at me, his eyes wide, his red hair lit up by the setting sun.

I stare out across the water. 'I can see crocodiles.'

'Caimans,' he says. 'We're not in Africa.'

'OK, caimans,' I say.

Red leans out and watches them. He sees them moving beneath the water, their bodies leaving ripples and trails of bubbles on the surface.

'Come on,' I say.

Red's hands grip the other oar and we row together, moving further out across the lagoon of dark green water. The ripples run outwards and gurgle through the tangle of mangrove roots.

Scarlet Ibis

Beyond the tree line, the mountains of the Northern Range rise up into the blue dusk sky.

'Look, Red,' I say. My voice is hushed in whisper. 'They're coming.'

Red stows the oars and sits next to me. This is the moment we have been waiting for. He sees them too. They drift like red smoke across the water. Only a few at first, but then more and more join them. We see them coming in their hundreds and thousands.

I pull Red's blanket up around him, so all I can see is his red hair and his eyes peeping out.

'We made it, Red,' I say. 'We made it, didn't we?'

Red leans back against me.

I wrap my arms around him and hug him tight.

We watch the scarlet ibis flying back to the Caroni Swamp.

We watch them settle in the trees, like bright red lanterns, as darkness falls.

Just Red and me in our little boat.

Just Red and me.

Together.

Dear Reader,

Sometimes a story forms from one strong idea that carries it, like a river running through the book. But some stories grow from many small ideas that begin as small streams and trickles that weave and thread together. Scarlet Ibis was inspired by many ideas and many people's stories, to become the story about Scarlet and her brother, Red.

There are many children like Scarlet living in the UK, children who have become the primary carers within their own families, often taking the adult role. These children have to juggle housework, cooking, and care of their siblings and parents as well as their own schoolwork. They miss their childhoods having to provide the practical and emotional support for their families at a time when they need that support themselves. Scarlet knows that if her mother's mental health deteriorates, she and Red may be separated and taken into care. For Scarlet, her family is all that she has, all she has ever known, and she desperately wants to keep her family together at whatever cost. Siblings taken into care are sometimes separated for reasons including the difficulty to keep large sibling groups together, or for an individual's specific health and emotional needs. For many children in care, the loss of contact with siblings has huge impact on the rest of their lives.

Birds form an important part of the story too. The empathy and connection Scarlet feels towards her brother is reflected in her care for a young pigeon. Pigeons have always fascinated me. Descended from rock doves, which lived on sea cliffs and mountain slopes, pigeons have come to live alongside us, our vertical buildings perfect substitutes for their natural habitats. Like us, they have adapted to an urban world. They have incredible navigation instincts too, and like many birds they can find their way across thousands of miles back home to their roosts. Scarlet ibis migrate daily between Trinidad and Venezuela, returning to the same trees in the Caroni Swamp each evening.

The initial idea for Scarlet Ibis began in the Caroni Swamp where I watched thousands of scarlet ibis returning to their evening roosts in the mangrove trees. I found Trinidad a fascinating country, a melting pot of different cultures, religions, and ethnic backgrounds. From the native Caribs and Arawaks, to Africans, Indians, Europeans, and Chinese who arrived during Trinidad's history of conquest, slavery, and immigration, the country is a vivid mix of people reflected in the music, food, and culture.

It made me think about the migration of people then and now, how humans, like birds have moved throughout the world either through choice or enforced displacement because of conflict or environmental changes. It made me question what we mean by identity, belonging, and home.

For me, my identity comes from the stories passed down through friends and family, from parents, grandparents, and great grandparents; from people who were farmers, miners, and steelworkers living in south Wales. These stories have become part of me, part of who I am. I wondered how I would feel if, like Scarlet and Red, I had no past to anchor me.

Yet, home and belonging are different to identity. I love the wild landscape of Wales. I feel a deep connection with it, but it does not feel like home. Home for me is not a physical place, but a place of belonging, through the friends and family I share my life with.

For Scarlet, the story she tells Red every night is her dream of home. Home for Scarlet isn't the Caroni Swamp. It is a place she and Red will always be together. Home really is where the heart is.

Gill Lewis, 2014

Do you love nature and wildlife? Here are Gill's top tips for getting involved

1. Join the Project Wild Thing movement. Take the Wild Time pledge and swap 30 minutes of screen time a day for 'wild time'. Find out more at **http://projectwildthing.com**.

2. Get outdoors. Check out the National Trust's list of 50 things to do before you're 11 ¾. Visit **www.nationaltrust.org.uk**. for more information.

3. Find your local Wildlife Trust by visiting **www.wildlifetrusts.org**. The Wildlife Trusts have a junior branch—Wildlife Watch—which has more than 150,000 members. If you care about nature and the environment and want to explore your local wildlife—this is the club for you! Their website also contains lots of free downloadable activities for things to make and do—visit **www.wildlifewatch.org.uk**.

4. Visit the RSPB website **www.rspb.org.uk** as well as the kids' page **www.rspb.org.uk/youth** to find games, activities, and information about how you can help Britain's wildlife.

5. Create a space for nature! It doesn't matter if you have a huge garden or a small window box—there is always room to allow for nature. Why not try growing wildflowers in a container pot? See the opposite page to find out how.

How to grow wildflowers in a container pot

What you need:
A plant pot with drainage holes in the bottom
Some ordinary garden soil or compost
Wildflower seed mix (this can be bought from most garden centres)
A little gravel (optional)
Water

What to do:
1. Fill a plant pot with ordinary garden soil or compost, leaving a space at the top for the seeds to go. You could also add a little gravel to help drainage.

2. Scatter the wildflower seed mix over the area and water gently.

3. Keep the soil damp until you start to see green shoots sprouting.

4. Place the pot in a sunny spot, and don't overwater.

5. Grow until it goes to seed. Save the seed and then use scissors to cut the stems to about 2 centimetres high. Wait for the following year's flowers . . .

Acknowledgements

Many of the social issues in this book are varied and far-reaching. It was never my intention to try to cover all these issues; indeed it would have been impossible. Instead, I have tried to touch on aspects relevant to this story. However, I could not have written it without the knowledge and experience generously shared by many professionals in this field. I would like to say a special thank you to Val and Penny for giving up their time to answer questions and to read through the first draft. Most of all, I would like to say a huge thank you to Gracie and Jacob who shared their stories with me. It's wonderful to know some stories really do have happy endings.

Gill Lewis spent much of her childhood in the garden where she ran a small zoo and a veterinary hospital for creepy-crawlies, mice, and birds. When she grew up she became a real vet and travelled from the Arctic to Africa in search of interesting animals and places.

Gill now writes books for children. Her first three novels, *Sky Hawk, White Dolphin, and Moon Bear* published to worldwide critical acclaim and have been translated into many languages.

She lives in the depths of Somerset with her husband and three children and writes from a tree house in the company of squirrels.

Sky Hawk

I set off over the back of the hill to the loch in the next valley.

Iona was waiting for me.

'You came then,' she said.

We were standing at the spot where I'd followed her footprints into the wood.

I nodded. 'So what's the secret?'

'You'll find out,' said Iona.

'It'd better be good,' I said.

She turned and headed into the wood.

The pines gave way to oak and birch and wild cherry. I thought I knew every inch of this farm. I'd grown up here. I'd built dens with Rob and Euan all over it. But this path through the trees looked different.

Iona stopped at the edge of a clearing. A ring of large boulders lay in a wide circle in the sunlit space. I leaned against one and pulled some damp moss with my fingers. The pale stone underneath was bright in the spring sunshine. I could imagine this was once a meeting place for the ancient Scottish Warrior Kings.

Iona put her finger to her lips for me to be quiet. 'Fairy stones,' she whispered.

'Fairy stones!' I said. 'You've brought me all this way just to see fairy stones?'

Iona giggled. 'Shh! Don't you believe in fairies, Callum?'

I scowled at her. 'I'm going home.'

Iona leaned against the trunk of a tree. It looked as if she was trying not to laugh. She tapped her fingers on the bark. 'Can you climb?' she asked.

I looked up into the tree. It was an old oak that had been struck by lightning some years before. The split trunk looked like a jagged scar against the sky. The nearest branches were beyond arms' reach and the bark was damp and fringed with moss.

'Climb that?' I snapped. 'Course I can.'

Iona kicked off her trainers and slid her fingers and toes into the tiny cracks in the bark. In no time, she had pulled herself up into the fork of branches above.

'Well, are you coming?'

I tried to grip the tree trunk, tried to wedge my feet onto the small ridges of bark, but each time my feet and hands slid. I looked up, but Iona had disappeared further up the tree.

'Iona!' I called. The end of a thick knotted rope fell by my feet. I hauled myself up into the tree and climbed higher to a natural platform of spreading branches. It was like a hidden fortress. You couldn't see it from the ground.

Iona had made seats from old crates and there were tins and boxes and an old hurricane lamp balanced in the tree. From there, I could see across the narrow waters of the loch to the mountains and the wide blue sky beyond.

'It's brilliant,' I said, 'brilliant.'

'Shh, you've got to be quiet,' she said. She pulled a canvas bag out from the hollow trunk and spilled out a blanket, an old leather case, and a packet of biscuits.

'I promise I won't tell anyone about this,' I whispered.

She threw me a biscuit and stifled a laugh. 'This isn't the secret, dummy. It's better than this, a million times better.'

I stuffed the biscuit in my mouth. 'What is it then?'

She pointed to a cluster of Scots pine-trees on the island not far from the shore. The tall bare trunks were crowned by a spread of branches, dense with green pine needles. From our platform of crates, we were level with the flattened tree tops.

'What's so special?' I said.

'Open your eyes, Callum,' said Iona. 'Look!'

I still couldn't see what she was pointing at. A pile of sticks lay on the topmost branches, like driftwood stacked on a high tide.

But something was moving inside. Something was

pulling the sticks into place. It wasn't just a random heap of twigs and branches. Something was building it.

And then I saw it.

I saw the secret hidden in our valley. No one else knew about it. Not Mum or Dad, or Graham, or Rob and Euan.

Just me, and Iona.

'Amazing isn't it?' whispered Iona.

I just nodded.

I was lost for words.

READ THE REST NOW . . .

Sky Hawk

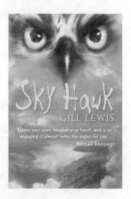